RAW GOLD

Bertrand W. Sinclair

HICKS DREW HIS AND SLAPPED ME OVER THE HEAD WITH
IT, EVEN AS MY FINGER CURLED ON THE TRIGGER.

RAW GOLD

A NOVEL

BY

BERTRAND W. SINCLAIR

Illustrations by
CLARENCE H. ROWE

CONTENTS

ILLUSTRATIONS

Hicks drew his and slapped me over the head with it, even as my
finger curled on the trigger   *Frontispiece*

Bedded in the soft earth underneath lay the slim buckskin sacks

"There's been too much blood shed over that wretched gold already.
Let them have it"

A war for the open road against an enemy whose only weapon was
his unswerving bulk

CHAPTER I.

THE LONG ARM OF THE LAW.

How many of us, I wonder, can look back over the misty, half-forgotten years and not see a few that stand out clear and golden, sharp-cut against the sky-line of memory? Years that we wish we could live again, so that we might revel in every full-blooded hour. For we so seldom get the proper focus on things until we look at them through the clarifying telescope of Time; and then one realizes with a pang that he can't back-track into the past and take his old place in the passing show.

Would we, if we could? It's an idle question, I know; wise men and musty philosophers say that regrets are foolish. But I speak for myself only when I say that I would gladly wheedle old, gray-bearded *Tempus* into making the wheels click backward till I could see again the buffalo-herds darkening the green of Northwestern prairies. They and the blanket Indian have passed, and the cowpuncher and Texas longhorns that replaced them will soon be little more than a vivid memory. Already the man with the plow is tearing up the brown sod that was a stamping-ground for each in turn; the wheat-fields have doomed the sage-brush, and truck-farms line the rivers where the wild cattle and the elk came down to drink.

It was a big life while it lasted — primitive, exhilarating, spiced with dangers that added zest to the game; the petty, sordid things of life only came in on the iron trail. There was no place for them in the old West, the dead-and-gone West that will soon be forgotten.

I expect nearly everybody between the Arctic Circle and the Isthmus of Panama has heard more or less of the Northwest Mounted Police. They're changing with the years, like everything else in this one-time buffalo country, but when Canada sent them out to keep law and order in a territory that was a City of Refuge for a lot of tough people who had played their string out south of the line, they were, as a dry old codger said about the Indian as a scalp-lifter, naturally fitted for

1

the task. And it was no light task, then, for six hundred men to keep the peace on a thousand miles of frontier.

It doesn't seem long ago, but it was in '74 that they filed down the gangway of a Missouri River boat, walking as straight and stiff as if every mother's son of them had a ramrod under his tunic, and out on a rickety wharf that was groaning under the weight of a king's ransom in baled buffalo-hides.

"Huh!" old Piegan Smith grunted in my ear. "Look at 'em, with their solemn faces. There'll be heaps uh fun in the Cypress Hills country when they get t' runnin' the whisky-jacks out. Ain't they a queer-lookin' bunch?"

They were a queer-looking lot to more than Piegan. Their uniforms fitted as if they had grown into them; scarlet jackets buttoned to the throat, black riding-breeches with a yellow stripe running down the outer seam of each leg, and funny little round caps like the lid of a big baking-powder can set on one side of their heads, held there by a narrow strap that ran around the chin. But for all their comic-opera get-up, there was many a man that snickered at them that day in Benton who learned later to dread the flash of a scarlet jacket on the distant hills.

They didn't linger long at Benton, but got under way and marched overland to the Cypress Hills. On Battle Creek they built the first post, Fort Walsh, and though in time they located others, Walsh remained headquarters for the Northwest so long as buffalo-hunting and the Indian trade endured. And Benton and Walsh were linked together by great freight-trails thereafter, for the Mounted Police supplies came up the Missouri and traveled by way of long bull-trains to their destination; there was no other way then; Canada was a wilderness, and Benton with its boats from St. Louis was the gateway to the whole Northwest.

Two years from the time Fort Walsh was built the La Pere outfit sent me across the line in charge of a bunch of saddle-horses the M. P. quartermaster had said he'd buy if they were good. I turned them over the afternoon I reached Walsh, and inside of forty-eight hours I was headed home with the sale-money—ten thousand dollars—in big bills, so that I could strap it round my middle. I remember that on the hill south of the post the three of us, two horse-wranglers and myself, flipped a dollar to see whether we kept to the Assiniboine trail or struck across country. It was a mighty simple transaction, but it produced some startling results for me, that same coin-spinning. The eagle came uppermost, and the eagle meant the open prairie for us. So we aimed for Stony Crossing, and let our horses jog; there were three of us, well mounted, and we had plenty of grub on a pack-horse; it seemed that our homeward trip should be a pleasant jaunt. It certainly never entered my head that I should soon have ample opportunity to see how high the "Riders of the Plains" stacked up when they undertook to enforce Canadian law and keep intact the peace and dignity of the Crown.

We had started early that morning, and by the time we thought of camping for dinner we saw ahead of us what we could tell was a white man's camp. It wasn't far, so we kept on, and presently it developed that we had accidentally come upon old Piegan Smith. He was lying there ostensibly resting his stock from the hard buffalo-running of the past winter, but I knew the old rascal's horses were more weary from a load of moonshine whisky they had lately jerked into the heart of the territory. But he was there, anyway, and half a dozen choice spirits with him, and when we'd said "Howdy" all around they proceeded to spring a keg of whisky on us.

Now, the whole Northwest groaned beneath a cast-iron prohibition law at that time, and for some years thereafter. No booze of any description was supposed to be sold in that portion of the Queen's domain. If you got so thirsty you couldn't stand it any longer, you could petition the governing power of the Territory for what was known as a "permit," which same document granted you leave and license to have in your possession one gallon of whisky. If you were a person of irreproachable character, and your humble petition reached his excellency when he was amiably disposed, you might, in the course of a few weeks, get the desired permission—but, any way you figured it, whisky was hard to get, and when you got it it came mighty high.

Naturally, that sort of thing didn't appeal to many of the high-stomached children of fortune who ranged up and down the Territory—being nearly all Americans, born with the notion that it is a white man's incontestable right to drink whatever he pleases whenever it pleases him. Consequently, every mother's son of them who knew how rustled a "worm," took up his post in some well-hidden coulée close to the line, and inaugurated a small-sized distillery. Others, with less skill but just as much ambition, delivered it in four-horse loads to the traders, who in turn "boot-legged" it to whosoever would buy. Some of them got rich at it, too; which wasn't strange, when you consider that everybody had a big thirst and plenty of money to gratify it. I've seen barrels of moonshine whisky, so new and rank that two drinks of it would make a jack-rabbit spit in a bull-dog's face, sold on the quiet for six and seven dollars a quart—and a twenty-dollar gold piece was small money for a gallon.

All this, of course, was strictly against the peace and dignity of the powers that were, and so the red-coated men rode the high divides with their eagle eye peeled for any one who looked like a whisky-runner. And whenever they did locate a man with the contraband in his possession, that gentleman was due to have his outfit confiscated and get a chance to ponder the error of his ways in the seclusion of a Mounted Police guardhouse if he didn't make an exceedingly fast getaway.

We all took a drink when these buffalo-hunters produced the "red-eye." So far as the right or wrong of having contraband whisky was concerned, I don't think any one gave it a second thought. The patriarchal decree of the government was a good deal of a joke on the plains, anyway—except when you were caught defying it! Then Piegan Smith set the keg on the ground by the fire where everybody could help himself as he took the notion, and I laid down by a wagon while dinner was being cooked.

After six weeks of hard saddle-work, it struck me just right to lie there in the shade with a cool breeze fanning my face, and before long I was headed smoothly for the Dreamland pastures. I hadn't dozed very long when somebody scattered my drowsiness with an angry yelp, and I raised up on one elbow to see what was the trouble.

Most of the hunters were bunched on one side of the fire, and they were looking pretty sour at a thin, trim-looking Mounted Policeman who was standing with his back to me, holding the whisky-keg up to his nose. A little way off stood his horse, bridle-reins dragging, surveying the little group with his ears pricked up as if he, too, could smell the whisky. The trooper sniffed a moment and set the keg down.

"Gentlemen," he asked, in a soft, drawly voice that had a mighty familiar note that puzzled me, "have you a permit to have whisky in your possession?"

Nobody said a word. There was really nothing they could say. He had them dead to rights, for it was smuggled whisky, and they knew that policeman was simply asking as a matter of form, and that his next move would be to empty the refreshments on the ground; if they got rusty about it he *might* haze the whole bunch of us into Fort Walsh—and that meant each of us contributing a big, fat fine to the Queen's exchequer.

"You know the law," he continued, in that same mild tone. "Where is your authority to have this stuff?"

Then the clash almost came. If old Piegan Smith hadn't been sampling the contents of that keg so industriously he would never have made a break. For a hot-tempered, lawless sort of an old reprobate, he had good judgment, which a man surely needed if he wanted to live out his allotted span in the vicinity of the forty-ninth parallel those troubled days. But he'd put enough of the fiery stuff under his belt to make him touchy as a parlor-match, and when the trooper, getting no answer, flipped the keg over on its side and the whisky trickled out among the grass-roots, Piegan forgot that he was in an alien land where the law is upheld to the last, least letter and the arm of it is long and unrelenting.

"Here's my authority, yuh blasted runt," he yelled, and jerked his six-shooter to a level with the policeman's breast. "Back off from that keg, or I'll hang your hide to dry on my wagon-wheel in a holy minute!"

CHAPTER II.

A REMINISCENT HOUR.

The policeman's shoulders stiffened, and he put one foot on the keg. He made no other move; but if ever a man's back was eloquent of determination, his was. From where I lay I could see the fingers of his left hand shut tight over his thumb, pressing till the knuckles were white and the cords in the back of his hand stood out in little ridges. I'd seen *that* before, and I recalled with a start when and where I'd heard that soft, drawly voice. I knew I wasn't mistaken in the man, though his face was turned from me, and I likewise knew that old Piegan Smith was nearer kingdom come than he'd been for many a day, if he did have the drop on the man with the scarlet jacket. He was holding his pistol on a double back-action, rapid-fire gun-fighter, and only the fact that Piegan was half drunk and the other performing an impersonal duty had so far prevented the opening of a large-sized package of trouble. While on the surface Smith had all the best of it, he needed that advantage, and more, to put himself on an even footing with Gordon MacRae in any dispute that had to be arbitrated with a Colt; for MacRae was the cool-headed, virile type of man that can keep his feet and burn powder after you've planted enough lead in his system to sink him in swimming water.

There was a minute of nasty silence. Smith glowered behind his cocked pistol, and the policeman faced the frowning gun, motionless, waiting for the flutter of Piegan's eye that meant action. The gurgling keg was almost empty when he spoke again.

"Don't be a fool, Smith," he said quietly. "You can't buck the whole Force, you know, even if you managed to kill me. You know the sort of orders we have about this whisky business. Put up your gun."

Piegan heard him, all right, but his pistol never wavered. His thin lips were pinched close, so tight the scrubby beard on his chin stood straight out in front; his chest was heaving, and the angry blood stood darkly red under his tanned cheeks. Altogether, he looked as if his trigger finger might crook without warning. It was one of those long moments that makes a fellow draw his breath sharp when he thinks about it afterward. If any one had made an unexpected move just then, there would have been sudden death in that camp. And while the lot of us sat and stood about perfectly motionless, not daring to say a word one way or the other, lest the wrathful old cuss squinting down the gun-barrel *would* shoot, the policeman took his foot off the empty cause of the disturbance, and deliberately turning his back on Piegan's leveled six-shooter, walked calmly over to his waiting horse.

Smith stared after him, frankly astonished. Then he lowered his gun. "The nerve uh the darned — —Say! don't go off mad," he yelled, his anger evaporating, changing on the instant to admiration for the other's cold-blooded courage. "Yuh spilled all the whisky, darn yuh—but then I guess yuh don't know any better'n t' spoil good stuff that away. No hard feelin's, anyhow. Stop an' eat dinner with us, an' we'll call it square."

The policeman withdrew his foot from the stirrup and smiled at Piegan Smith, and Piegan, to show that his intentions were good, impulsively unbuckled his cartridge-belt and threw belt and six-shooters on the ground.

"I don't hanker for trouble with a *hombre* like you," he grunted. "I guess I was a little bit hasty, anyhow."

"I call you," the policeman said, and stripping the saddle and bridle from his sweaty horse, turned him loose to graze.

"Hello, Mac!" I hailed, as he walked up to the fire. He turned at the sound of my voice with vastly more concern than he'd betrayed under the muzzle of Piegan's gun.

"Sarge himself!" he exclaimed. "Beats the devil how old trails cross, eh?"

"It sure does," I retorted, and our hands met.

He sat down beside me and began to roll a cigarette. You wouldn't call that a very demonstrative greeting between two old *amigos* who'd bucked mesquite and hair-lifting Comanches together, all over the Southwest. It had been many a moon since we took different roads, but MacRae hadn't changed that I could see. That was his way—he never slopped over, no matter how he felt. If ever a mortal had a firm grip on his emotions, MacRae had, and yet there was a sleeping devil within him that was never hard to wake. But his looks gave no hint of the real man under the surface placidity; you'd never have guessed what possibilities lay behind that immobile face, with its heavy-lashed hazel eyes and plain, thin-lipped mouth that tilted up just a bit at the corners. We had parted in the Texas Panhandle five years before—an unexpected, involuntary separation that grew out of a poker game with a tough crowd. The tumultuous events of that night sent me North in undignified haste, for I am not warlike by nature, and Texas was no longer healthy for me unless I cared to follow up a bloody feud. But I'd left Mac a trail-boss for the whitest man in the South, likewise engaged to the finest girl in any man's country; and it's a far cry from punching cows in Texas to wearing the Queen's colors and keeping peace along the border-line. I knew, though, that he'd tell me the how and why of it in his own good time, if he meant that I should know.

One or two of the buffalo-hunters exchanged words with us while Mac was building his cigarette and lighting it. Old Piegan stretched himself in the grass, and in a few moments was snoring energetically, his grizzled face bared to the cloudless sky. The camp grew still, except for the rough and ready cook pottering about the fire, boiling buffalo-meat and mixing biscuit-dough. The fire crackled around the Dutch ovens, and the odor of coffee came floating by. Then Mac hunched himself against a wagon-wheel and began to talk.

"I suppose it looks odd to you, Sarge, to see me in this rig?" he asked whimsically. "It beats punching cows, though—that is, when a fellow discovers that he isn't a successful cowpuncher."

"Does it?" I returned dryly. "You were making good in the cow business last time I saw you. What did you see in the Mounted Police that took your fancy?"

He shrugged his shoulders philosophically. "They're making history in this neck of the woods," he said, "and I joined for lack of something better to do. You'll find us a cosmopolitan lot, and not bad specimens as men go. It's a tolerably satisfying life—once you get out of the ranks."

"How about that?" I queried; and as I asked the question I noticed for the first time the gilt bars on his coat sleeve. "You've got past the buck trooper stage then? How long have you been in the force?"

"Joined the year they took over the Territory," he replied. "Yes, I've prospered in the service. Got to be a sergeant; I'm in charge of a line-post on Milk River—Pend d' Oreille. You'd better come on over and stay with me a day or two, Sarge."

"I was heading in that direction," I answered, "only I expected to cross the river farther up. But, man, I never thought to see you up here. I thought you'd settled down for keeps; supposed you were playing major-domo for the Double R down on the Canadian River, and the father of a family by this time. How we do get switched around in this old world."

"Don't we, though," he said reflectively. "It's a great game. You never know when nor where your trail is liable to fork and lead you to new countries and new faces, or maybe plumb over the big divide. Oh, well, it'll be all the same a hundred years from now, as Bill Frayne used to say."

"You've turned cynic," I told him, and he smiled.

"No," he declared, "I rather think I'd be classed as a philosopher; if you could call a man a philosopher who can enjoy hammering over this bald country, chasing up whisky-runners and hazing non-treaty Indians onto reservations, and raising hell generally in the name of the law. Still, I don't take life as seriously as I used to. What's the use? We eat and drink and sleep and work and fight because it's the nature of us two-legged brutes; but there's no use getting excited about it, because things never turn out exactly the way you expect them to, anyhow."

"If that's your philosophy of life," I bantered, "you ought to make a rattling good policeman. I can see where a calm, dispassionate front would save a man a heap of trouble, at this sort of thing."

"Josh all you like," MacRae laughed, "but I tell you a man does save himself a heap of trouble when he doesn't get too anxious whether things come out just as he wants them to or not. Six or seven years ago I couldn't have done this sort of work. I've changed, I reckon. There was a time when I'd have felt that there was only one way to settle a row like I just had. And the chances are that I would have wound up by putting that old boy's light out. Which wouldn't have helped matters any for me, and certainly would have been tough on old Piegan Smith—who happens to be a pretty fair sort; only playing the opposite side of the game."

As if the low-spoken sound of his name had reached his ears and electrified him, Piegan sat up very suddenly, and at the same instant the cook sounded the long call. So we broke off our chat, and getting a tin plate and cup and a set of eating-implements, we helped ourselves from the Dutch ovens and squatted in the grass to eat.

When we'd finished, one of the hunters rounded up the horses and we caught our nags and saddled them. MacRae was going back to his post that night, and I also was in haste to be traveling—that ten thousand dollars of another man's money was a responsibility I wanted to be rid of without the least possible delay. Pend d' Oreille was twenty-five or thirty miles south of us—a long afternoon's ride, but MacRae and I were glad of each other's company, and it was worth while straining a point to have even one night's shelter at a Police camp in that semi-hostile country. There were no road-agents to speak of, for sums of money large enough to tempt gentry of that ilk seldom passed over those isolated trails; but here and there stray parties of Stonies and Blackfeet, young bucks in war-paint and breech-clout, hot on the trail of their first medicine, skulked warily among the coulée-scarred ridges, keeping in touch with the drifting buffalo-herds and alert for a chance to ambush a straggling white man and lift his hair. They weren't particularly dangerous, except to a lone man, still there was always the chance of running slap into them, in which case they usually made a more or less vigorous attempt to wipe you out. A red coat, however, was a passport to safety; even so early in the game the copper-colored brother had learned that the Mounted Police were a hard combination—an enemy who never turned back when he took the war-trail.

When we were mounted Mac leaned over and muttered an admonitory word for Piegan's ear alone. "Better lay low, Smith," he said, "and let the boot-leggers go it on their own hook for a while. We are watching for you. It's only a matter of time till somebody takes you in, because your whisky is making lots of nasty work for us these days, and we've got orders from the big chief to nail you if there's a show. I'm passing up this little affair to-day. That doesn't count. But the next time you cross the river with a four-horse load of it I'll be on you like a wolf. If I don't, some other fellow will. *Sabe?* Think it over."

Smith bit off a huge chew of tobacco, while he digested MacRae's warning. Then he looked up with a smile that broadened to a grin. "You're all right," he said cheerfully. "I like your style. If I get the worst of the deal, I won't holler. So-long!"

CHAPTER III.

BIRDS OF PREY.

Once clear of the buffalo-hunters' camp, MacRae and I paired off and speedily began to compare notes, where we had been, what we had done, how the world had used us in the five years since we had seen each other last. And although we gabbled freely enough, MacRae avoided all mention of the persons of whom I most wished to hear. I didn't press him, for I knew that something out of the common must have happened, else he would not have been wearing the Queen's scarlet, and I didn't care to bring up a subject that might prove a sore one with him. But men we had known and trails we had followed furnished us plenty of grist for the conversational mill. Our talk ranged from the Panhandle to the Canada line, while our horses jogged steadily southward.

Dark came down on the four of us as we topped Manyberries Ridge, and seven or eight miles of rolling prairie still lay between us and Pend d' Oreille. If Mac had been alone he would have made the post by sundown, for the Mounted Police rode picked horses, the best money could buy. But it was a long jaunt to Benton, and the rest of us were inclined to an easier pace, that we might husband the full strength of our grass-fed mounts for any emergency that should arise on the way.

With the coming of night a pall of clouds blew out of the west, blanketing the stars and shutting off their hazy light completely, and when the sky was banked full from horizon to horizon, the dark enveloped us like a black sea-mist. Once or twice we startled a little bunch of buffalo, and listened to the thud of their hoofs as they fled through the sultry, velvet gloom; but for the most our ride was attended by no sounds save the night song of frogs in the upland sloughs and the hollow clank of steel bits keeping time to the creak of saddle-leather.

Halfway down the long slope MacRae and I, riding in the lead, pulled up to make a cigarette on the brink of a straight-walled coulée that we could sense but not see. As I waited for Mac to strike a match my eyes roved about, seeking to pierce the unnatural blackness that wrapped itself about us, and while my gaze was for an instant fixed on the night-enshrouded canyon, a red tongue of flame flashed out for a moment in the inky shadow below. MacRae saw it also, and held the match unstruck.

"Must be somebody camped down there," I hazarded.

"A camp-fire would hardly flash and die out like that, Sarge," he answered thoughtfully. "At least, not an ordinary one. There are some folk in this country, you know, who manifest a very retiring disposition at times. That looks to me like a blind fire or a signal. Let's wait a minute."

We sat there on our horses, grouped close together, a minute that lengthened to five; then MacRae broke off in the middle of a sentence as the flare leaped up, flickered an instant, and was blotted out again. I could have sworn I heard a cry, and one of my men spoke in a tone that assured me my imagination had not been playing a trick.

"Hear that?" he asked eagerly. "Somebody hollered down there."

"I don't much like that," MacRae said, in a low tone. "I have a hunch that something crooked is going on, and I reckon I'll go down and see what that fire means. You fellows better go a little farther and wait for me."

"Not on your life," I protested. "You might run into most any kind of formation. We'll go in a bunch, if we go at all."

"Might be Injuns," Bruce Haggin put in. "An', anyhow, whatever play comes up, four men's a heap better'n one. If you're bound t' mix in, why, lead the way. I'm kinda curious about what's down there m'self."

So near to the post it was that MacRae almost knew the feel of the ground underfoot. He led us a hundred yards along the rim of the bank and stopped again.

"This is as good a place as any, but you'll have to get down and lead your horses," he warned. "It's a devil of a scramble from here to the bottom."

We dismounted, and speedily found that MacRae hadn't exaggerated the evil qualities of that descent. If there had been boulders on that hillside the noise of our coming would have alarmed a deaf man; but the soft dirt and slippery grass gave out no sound, though we slid and tumbled and dug in our heels for a foothold till the sweat streamed down our cheeks.

At the bottom we mounted again and followed MacRae in a cautious file around clumps of willow and rustling quaking-asp to the place where the blaze should have shown. But no glint of fire appeared in any direction; the coulée-bottom lay more dark and silent, if that were possible, than the gloomy hills above. Perplexed, MacRae halted, and we bunched together, whispering, each of us straining his eyes and ears to catch some sight or sound of life in that black, ghostly quiet. We might have concluded that our senses had been playing pranks at our expense, that the flame we had seen from the ridge was purely an imaginary thing, but for the rank, unmistakable odor of burning wood—a smell no man bred in a land of camp-fires can mistake. We were near it, wherever it was, but how near we had no means of knowing.

After a bit of waiting, Mac decided that the smoke was floating from a certain direction, and we began to edge carefully that way. Presently we circled a clump of brush, to come near riding right into a banked fire, barely visible, even at short range, under its covering of earth. A dimly outlined bulk lay beside it, and leaning over in our saddles, the faint glow of the coals revealed a man's body, half stripped of its clothing, and—oh, well, such things are so utterly devilish you wouldn't credit it. It's bad enough to kill, even when it's necessary; but I never could understand how a white man could take a leaf out of the Indian's torture-book.

The fire had been heaped over with earth—to screen it from prying eyes, I suppose, while the good work went on. We got off our horses and stooped over the man, forgetting for the moment that danger might lurk in the surrounding thicket. Mac swore under his breath when he bent and peered keenly at the man's face; then he straightened up and kicked a part of the clay covering from the smoldering embers. As the bright glow of a little cascade of sparks pierced the darkness, a voice in our rear called sharply: "Hands up!" and we swung round to behold two masked faces regarding us from behind steadily held Winchesters.

The very suddenness of the hold-up made it a complete success. Apart, and moving, we might have scattered in the brush like young quail, and so have been able to give the gentlemen a hard run for the money. But we were bunched together, shocked out of all caution, staring at the pitiful figure at our feet when MacRae unmasked the fire, and the flare of it surrounded us with a yellow nimbus that made us fair marks for a gun. With that dazzling light in our eyes and those ugly-looking customers at the business end of the guns, it would have been out and out suicide to reach for a six-shooter. For at that period in Northwestern history, when a man had the drop on you under such conditions, there was absolutely no question of what would happen if you made a suspicious move. We were fairly caught, and there was nothing to do but elevate our digits and paw the air as commanded.

It took one of those Western Turpins about a minute to relieve us of our artillery, after which he silently proceeded to lead our horses out of sight. When he did that I began to hope the horses were all they wanted, that they had no knowledge of the money I carried; but my hopes died an early death, for he was back in a moment, and the man behind the gun indicated me with a motion of the Winchester.

"That long, stoop-shouldered gazabo's got the stuff on him," he growled.

There was half a second when I entertained a wild notion of getting fractious. A fellow hates to make a bungle of the first decent trust he's had in a long time; but I was in a tight place, and I couldn't figure where I'd delay giving up beyond the length of time it would take the gentleman with the Winchester to drill me. Under the circumstances it didn't take long to decide that it was a heap better all around to be robbed alive than dead—they'd get the money anyway, and if I got myself shot up to no purpose that would spoil all chance of getting back at them later.

The silent partner wasted no time in fruitless search of my person. He seemed to know right where to look, which was another feature of the play that I didn't *sabe* at the time. He reached down inside my shirt, with a none too gentle hand, and relieved me of the belt that held the money. Then the pair of them backed up, still covering us, and faded away in the gloom.

CHAPTER IV.

A TALE HALF TOLD.

When they were gone we let our hands down to their natural level and drew a long breath.

"We appear to have got considerably the worst of this transaction," I observed. "The La Pere outfit is shy something like ten thousand dollars—we're afoot, minus everything but cigarette material. It's a wonder they didn't take that, too. A damn good stroke of business, all right," I finished, feeling mighty sore at myself. When it was too late, I could think of half a dozen ways we might have avoided getting held up.

"I got you into it, too," MacRae said calmly. "But don't get excited and run on the rope this early in the game, Sarge; you'll only throw yourself. Brace up. We've been in worse holes before." Never a word of what it might mean to him; never even hinted that the high moguls at Fort Walsh were more than likely to put him on the rack for letting any such lawless work be carried out successfully, in his own district. A Mounted Policeman can make no excuses for letting a tough customer slip through his fingers; the only way he can escape censure is to be brought in feet first.

He motioned to the poor devil lying by the fire.

"Look at him, Sarge," he went on, in a different tone. "You always had a pretty good memory for faces. So have I, for that matter, but—go ahead—look."

I bent over the man, looked closely at the still features, dropped on one knee and turned his face toward the firelight to make sure. I recognized him instantly, and I knew that MacRae had no doubts of his identity, for each of us had broken bread and slept in the same blankets with that quiet figure.

"It's Rutter," I whispered, and MacRae nodded silently.

"He's done for, too—no, by God, he isn't!" I cried, and shrank involuntarily, for his eyeballs rolled till only the whites showed in a way that made me shudder. "He's not dead, yet, Mac!"

"One of you fellows get some water," Mac commanded. He squatted beside me, holding up Rutter's head. In a minute Bruce was back with his hat full of water from the creek that whimpered just beyond the willow patch. I peeled off my coat and spread it over the marred limbs, and Bruce held the water so that I could dip in my hand and sprinkle Rutter's face. After a little his mouth began to twitch. Queer gurgling sounds issued from his throat. He moved his head slightly, looking from me to MacRae. Presently he recognized us both; his face brightened.

"Gimme a drink," he whispered huskily.

Mac propped him up so that he could sip from the hat. He came near going off again, but rallied, and in a second or two his lips framed a question:

"Did yuh—get 'em?"

I shook my head. "You might say that they got us," I answered.

"Who were they, Hans?" MacRae questioned eagerly. "And why did they do this to you? We'll make them sweat blood for this night's work. Did you know them? Tell us if you can."

"No," Rutter spoke with a great effort. Each sentence came as if torn piecemeal from his unwilling tongue; short, jerky phrases, conceived in pain and delivered in agony. "We—me'n Hank Rowan—comin' from the North—made a stake on the Peace. They started it—at the Stone—yuh know—Writin'-Stone. Hank an' me—you'll find Hank in the cottonwoods—Stony Crossin'. I tried—tried t' make Walsh. Two of 'em—masked—tried t' make me tell—tell 'em—where we made the *cache*. I'm—I'm done—I guess. The dust, it's—it's—a-a-ah——"

The gnarled hands shut up into clenched fists, and the feeble voice trailed off in an agonized moan.

I laved his pain-twisted face with the cool water and let a few drops trickle into his open mouth. He gasped a few times, then, gathering strength again, went on with that horrible spasmodic recitation.

"They were after us—a long time. Lyn's at Walsh. There's a—a good stake. Get it—for her. It's *cached*—under the Stone—yuh know—Writin'-Stone. Three sacks. That's what—they wanted. You'll—you'll—on the rock above—marked—gold—raw gold—that's it—gold—raw gold—Mac—I want—I want——"

That was all. The tense muscles relaxed. His head fell back limp on MacRae's arm, and the rest of the message went with the game old Dutchman across the big divide. We laid him down gently, folded his arms on his breast, and for a moment held our peace in tribute to his passing.

MacRae was first to speak.

"There's a lot back of this that I can't understand," he said, more to himself than to the rest of us. "It beats me why these two old cowmen should be here in this country, tangled up with buried gold-dust, and being hunted like beasts for its possession. Old Hans was certainly in his right mind or he wouldn't have known us; and if he told us right, Hank Rowan has been murdered too. If Lyn is at Walsh, she may be able to shed some light on this. But I'll swear I feel like a man groping in a dark room."

"If Lyn is at Walsh," I asserted stoutly, "she got there since I left this morning. I was there two days, and I wasn't in the background by any means; and she's the sort of girl that isn't backward about hailing a friend. We know one thing—the men that killed Rutter are the ones that held us up, and got off with that money of mine. And say—how did those fellows know I had that money and where I was carrying it? Good Lord! it sounds like the plot of a dime novel."

It was a stubborn riddle for us to try and read. And our surroundings at that particular moment were not the most favorable to coherent thought or plausible theory-building. When a man has been robbed at the point of a gun, and set afoot in the heart of an unpeopled waste, with a dead man and a dying fire for company, his nerves are apt to get a little bit on edge. Things that wouldn't tax your fortitude in daylight look like the works of the devil when you have to face them in the black hours of the night. None of us are so far removed from savagery that a few grains of superstition don't lurk in our souls, all ready to bob up if the setting is appropriate. If it should ever be my lot to take the Long Trail at short notice, I hope it will be under a blue sky and a blazing sun. It was hard to be philosophic, or even decently calm, standing there in the sickly glow of the fading coals with old Hans mutely reminding us that life is a tenuous thread, easily snipped.

A little night breeze rustling the willows about us brought into my mind the fact that our masked acquaintances could easily sneak up and pot us if, as an afterthought, they decided to do a really workmanlike job. Doubt it? Wasn't the dead man stretched in the shadow convincing proof of their capacity for pure devilishness? Read the history of those days along the line, and you'll turn some red pages. There were no half-way measures in the code of an outlaw then; the pair who held us up would have taken our lives as nonchalantly as they relieved us of our material possessions had we proved in the least degree troublesome.

I hinted what was in my mind to MacRae, and when he agreed that it was a possible contingency, we filed out of the treacherous light and squatted in the edge of a quaking-asp grove where we couldn't be seen, and where a coyote, much less a man, couldn't steal up on us without the crackle of dry brush betraying him.

"What do you think you'll do, Sarge?" Mac whispered to me, while we sat there undecided as to our next move. "Go on to Benton, or stay here on the chance of breaking even?"

"I've got to stick; it's the only thing I can do," I growled back. "I've been sure enough whipsawed this deal, but I'm still in the game, and when it comes to calling the last turn I'll be there with a stack of blues. How in hell can I show my face in Benton while some other fellow is packing the money La Pere trusted me to bring back? If I can rustle horses I'll send these two boys on home, with a note to the old man explaining how the play came up. If those jaspers flash any part of the roll in the Territory before snowfall, I'll get them. I've got to get them, to square myself."

"That would be my idea, if I were in your place," he answered. "If they're like the average run of men that turn a trick of that kind, they'll give themselves away in the long run. It's lucky, in a way, that you had paper money instead of gold; the big bills will be their downfall if they undertake to spend them in this country—and if old Hans had it straight, they're not going to pull out with a measly ten thousand dollars. It's an ugly mess, and liable to be worse before it's cleaned up. If there is a stake like that *cached* around the Stone, these land pirates will camp mighty close on the trail of anybody that goes looking for it. And it won't be any Sunday-school picnic dealing with them—they showed a strong hand there," he motioned to the place where Rutter lay.

"The best thing we can do," he continued, "is to drag it for Pend d' Oreille, afoot. We have two extra horses there. We can get a little sleep and move early in the morning. I'll have to report this thing in person at Walsh, but before I do I want to know if Hank Rowan was really killed at Stony Crossing. If we find him there as Rutter said, you can gamble that trouble has camped in our dooryard for a lengthy stay. And it might be a good idea for you to give your men a gentle hint to keep their mouths closed about this affair—all of it. There's a slim chance at the best of finding that gold, even if it's there, and it won't help us nor the rest of the Force to run down the men who held us up, if everybody on both sides of the line gets to talking about it."

"I'll tell them," I agreed. "I reckon you have the right idea. I think it's a cinch that if we land the men that set us afoot and got away with the money, we'll have the cold-blooded brutes that put Hans Rutter's light out. But I don't *sabe*, Mac, why those old-timers should be mixed into a deal of this kind. Their cattle and range on the Canadian had a gold-mine beat to death for money-making; old men like them don't jump two thousand miles from home without mighty strong reasons."

"They probably had, if we only knew," MacRae muttered. "I reckon we'd better start; we can't do any good here."

Mac led the way. The four of us slipped through the brushy bottom as silently as men unaccustomed to walking might go, for we had no hankering, unarmed as we were, to bring those red-handed marauders after us again, if they happened to be lurking in that canyon. Rutter's body we had no choice but to leave undisturbed by the blackening fire. In the morning we would come back and bury him, but for that night—well, he was beyond any man's power to aid or injure, lying there alone in the dark.

CHAPTER V.

MOUNTED AGAIN.

We stumbled along, close up, for the thick-piled clouds still hung their light-obscuring banners over the sky. Three yards apart we became invisible to each other. I followed behind MacRae more or less mechanically, though I was, in a way, acutely conscious of the necessity for stealthy going, one part of my mind busy turning over the quick march of events and guessing haphazard at the future.

Striding along in this mental semi-detachment from the business in hand, some three hundred yards down the coulée I tripped over a fallen cottonwood and drove the point of a projecting limb clean through the upper of my boot and into the calf of my leg—not a disabling wound, but one that lacked nothing in the way of pain. The others stopped while I pulled out the snag, which had broken off the trunk, and while I was about this a familiar clattering noise uprose near-by. Ever hear a horse shake himself, like a water-spaniel fresh from a dip, when he has been tied for a long time in one place with the dead weight of a heavy stock saddle on his back? There is a little by-play of grunting and clearing of nostrils, then the slap of skirts and strings and stirrup-leathers—a man never forgets or mistakes the sound of it, if he has ever slept in a round-up camp with a dozen restless night-horses saddled and tied to a wagon twenty feet from his bed. But it made us jump, welling up out of the dark so unexpectedly and so near.

"Saddle-horse—tied," Mac tersely commented. We squatted in the long grass and buck-brush, listening, and a few seconds later heard a horse snort distinctly. This sound was immediately followed by the steady beat of an impatient forefoot.

"Over yonder," I said. "And there's more than one, I think. Let's investigate this. And we'd better not separate."

Fifty yards to the left we struck a cottonwood grove, and in the outer edge of it loomed the vague outline of a horse—when we were almost within reaching-distance of him. I ran my hand over the saddle and knew it instantly for Bruce Haggin's rig. A half-minute of quiet prowling revealed our full quota of livestock, even to the pack-horse that bore our beds and grub, each one tied hard and fast to a tree. Also our six-shooters reposed in their scabbards, the four belts hooked over the horn of MacRae's saddle.

Maybe it didn't feel good to be on the hurricane deck of a good horse once more! Whenever I have to walk any distance, I can always understand why a horse-thief yields to temptation and finally becomes confirmed in his habit. It was rather an odd thing for those outlaws to leave everything, even to our guns, but I figured—and time proved the correctness of my arithmetic—that they had bigger fish to fry.

Once in the saddle, with the comfortable weight of a cartridge-belt around each man's middle, we experienced a revulsion of feeling. Primed for trouble if we could jump it out of the brush, we rode the bottom for half an hour. But our men were gone. At least, we could not locate them. So we took to the upland again and loped toward Pend d' Oreille.

"I've been thinking it isn't so strange—those old fellows being in this country—after all," Mac suddenly began, as we slowed our horses down to take a hill. "I didn't remember at first, but two years ago, just after I joined the Force, I ran across a bull-whacker on the Whoop Up trail, and he told me that the Double R had closed out. He said Hank had got into a ruction with Dick Feltz—you recollect there was considerable feeling between them in our time down there—and killed him one day at Fort Worth. Feltz had some folks that took it up, and Hank had to spend a barrel of money to come clear. That, and a range war that grew out of the killing, and some kind of a business deal just about broke them. That's the way this fellow had it; said a trail-boss told him at Ogalalla that spring. I didn't take much stock in the yarn at the time, but I'm beginning to think he had it straight. You didn't hear anything about it?"

"Not a word; it's news to me," I said. "When I left that country I kept moving north all the time. The last three years I've been in the Judith Basin, and southern outfits haven't begun to come in there yet. So I haven't had much chance to hear from that part of the world. But I'm framing up my think-works so I won't be surprised at anything I see or hear after to-night. How long since you left that country, Mac?"

"Next spring after you did," he answered. "If they did go broke, I can *sabe* their being here. Rutter said, you know, that they'd made a stake on the Peace—Peace River, I suppose he meant. There's been a lot of placer mining in that north country the last three or four years. They might have been up there and struck it good and plenty. They made their start in the cow business off a placer in California, you know."

I knew that, for Rowan often spoke of it. And granting that we had surmised rightly, it required no vivid imagination to picture what might happen to men crossing those wide prairies with a fortune in yellow dust. But my imagination was hardly equal to the task of reconciling the fact that the evil pair had been busy at other deviltry and yet knew I carried a large sum of money and where it was concealed about my person. That brought me back to something else Rutter had told us; something that I knew—or thought I knew—touched MacRae very closely.

"Hans said Lyn was at Walsh," I remarked. "I don't think she was there, this morning. But she might be due to arrive there. Hang it all, Mac, what the dickens chased you away from the Canadian?"

"Looking back, I can't just say what it was," he presently replied, in a hard, matter-of-fact tone. "You see, one's feelings can change, Sarge. It looks different to me now than it did then. I reckon I could have written essays on the futility of sentiment, and the damned silliness of a man who thinks he cares for a woman. But I'm past that stage. And so I can't say for sure just how it was or why. Something came up between me and Lyn—and I drifted, and kept drifting. Went through Colorado, Wyoming, Montana; finally rambled here, and went into the Force because—well, because a man with anything to him can go to the top. A man must play at something, and this looked like a good game."

There was a note of something that I'd never heard in MacRae's voice before; neither bitterness nor anger nor sorrow nor lonesomeness, and yet there was a hint of each, but so slight, so elusive I couldn't grasp it. I remembered that the last sentence MacRae had spoken to me in the South was a message to Lyn Rowan, a message that I never had the pleasure of delivering, for my hasty flitting took me out other trails than the one that led to the home ranch. And so they had parted—gone different ways— probably in anger. Well, that's only another example of the average human's cussedness. Lyn could be just as haughty as she was sweet and gracious, which was natural enough, seeing she'd ruled a cattle king and all his sunburned riders since she was big enough to toddle alone; and Gordon MacRae wasn't the sort of man who would come to heel at any woman's bidding—at least, he wasn't in the old days. Oh, I could understand how it happened, all right. Each of them was chuck full of that dubious sort of pride that has busted up more than one love-*fiesta*.

Neither of us spoke again, and at length the squat log buildings of Pend d' Oreille loomed ahead of us in the night. Tired and hungry, we stabled our horses, ate a bite, and rolled into bed.

CHAPTER VI.

STONY CROSSING.

"There's Stony Crossing, Sarge; and over yonder, at the west end of that blue ridge, is Writing-on-the-Stone."

At the foot of the long slope on which we stood Milk River glinted in the sunshine, deceptively beautiful—a shining example of the truth of that old saw about distance lending enchantment, for, looking down on the placid stream slipping smoothly along between fringes of scrubby timber, one would never guess that miles and miles of hungry quick-sands lined the river-edge, an unseen trap for the feet of the unwary.

Stony Crossing I could see, even without Mac's guiding finger. The Whoop Up trail, a brown streak against the vivid upland green, dipped down the hillside to our right, down to the sage-grown flat, and into the river by the great boulders that gave the ford its name. The blue ridge up the river I gave scant heed to; the Writing-Stone was only a name to me, for I'd never seen the place. My attention was all for the scene at hand. The patch of soft green that I knew for the cottonwoods Rutter had spoken of drew my roving gaze whether I would or no. I have ridden on pleasanter missions than the one that took us to Stony Crossing that day.

"It's sure tough," I voiced a thought that had been running in my mind all morning, "to think that a good old fellow like Hank Rowan has been murdered and left to rot on the prairie like a skinned buffalo. Hanged if I can make myself really believe we'll find him down there."

"The more I think of it, the more I'm inclined to believe that we will," MacRae answered evenly. "We'll know beyond a doubt in the next hour. So we might as well go on."

If I hadn't known him so well I might have thought he didn't care a damn what we found at Stony Crossing, that he was as unmoved as the two case-hardened troopers who rode with us. But that repression was just as natural to him as emotional flare-ups are to some. Whatever he felt he usually kept bottled up inside, no matter how it hurt. I never saw him fly to pieces over anything. He was something of an anomaly to me, when I first knew him. I was always so prone to do and say things according to impulse that I thought him cold-blooded, a man without any particular feeling except a certain pride in holding his own among his fellows.

But I revised my opinion when I came to know him better. Under the surface he was sensitive as a girl; one could wound him with a word or a look. Paradoxically, he was absolutely cold-blooded toward a declared enemy. He would fight fair, but without mercy. Side by side with the sensitive soul of him, and hidden always under an impassive mask of self-control, lay the battling spirit, an indomitable fighting streak; it cropped out in a cool, calculating manner of taking desperate chances when the sleeping devil in him was roused. He would sidestep trouble—and one met the weeping damsel at many turns of the road in those raw days—if he could do it without loss of self-respect; but the man who stirred him up needlessly, or crowded him into retaliation, always regretted it—when he had time to indulge in vain regrets. And you can bet your last, lone *peso*, and consider it won, that MacRae meant every word when he said to old Hans Rutter: "We'll make them sweat blood for this."

When we got down into the bottom Mac turned aside to the deep-worn trail and glanced sharply down at the ruts. The dust in them lay smooth, and the hoof-marks that showed were old and dim.

"I wondered if there had been any freight teams pass lately," he explained. "But there hasn't—not for a day or two, anyway. Let's look in the timber."

That was a long time ago, and since then I have seen much of life and death in many countries, but I can recall as distinctly as if it were yesterday the grim sight that met us when we rode in among the whispering cottonwoods. We found Hank Rowan in a little open place, where rifts of sunlight filtered through the tangled branches; one yellow bar, full of quivering motes, rested on the wide-open eyes and mouth, tinting the set features the ghastly color of a plaster cast. The horse he had ridden lay dead across his legs, and just beyond, a crumpled heap against the base of a tree, was the carcass of a mule, half-hidden under a bulky pack. The thing that sickened me, that stirs me even yet, was a circular, red patch that crowned his head where should have been thick, iron-gray hair.

"The damned hounds!" MacRae muttered. "They tried to make it look like an Indian job."

The pack-ropes had been cut and the pack searched. In the same manner they had gone through his pockets and scattered a few papers and letters on the ground. These we gathered carefully together, against the time of meeting Lyn, and then—for time pressed, and a dead man, though he may be your friend and his passing a sorrow, is out of the game forever—we dragged him from beneath the dead horse, wrapped him in the canvas pack-cover, and buried him in the soft leaf-mold where he lay, as we had buried his lifetime partner early in the morning. When we had finished, MacRae ordered his two troopers back to Pend d' Oreille, and we mounted our horses and turned their heads toward Fort Walsh.

It is seventy miles in an air-line from Stony Crossing to the fort. That night we laid out, sleeping without hardship in a dry buffalo-wallow, and noon of the next day brought us to Walsh, a huddle of log buildings clustering around a tall pole from which fluttered the union jack.

Off to one side of the fort a bunch of work-bulls fed peacefully. Down in the creek bottom a tent or two flapped in the mid-day breeze, and in their neighborhood uprose the smoke of half a dozen dinner fires. By the post storeroom, waiting their turn to unload, was ranged a line of the tarpaulin-covered wagons, wheeled galleons of the plains, that brought food and raiment to the Northwest before the coming of steam and steel.

"That looks to me like Baker's outfit, from Benton," I said to MacRae, as we swung off our horses before the building in which the officer of the day held forth. "They must have come by way of Assiniboine."

"Probably," Mac answered. "And over yonder's the paymaster's train. At least, he's due, and I can't account for a bunch of horses in charge of a buck trooper any other way."

We clanked into the ante-room—that's what I call it, anyway. It happened that I didn't stay around those police posts long enough to get familiar with the technical terms for everything. Not that they wouldn't have welcomed my presence; faith, their desire for my company was only equaled by my reluctance to accept their hospitality. There was a while when I developed a marvelous capacity for dodging invitations to Fort Walsh. And if the men in scarlet had been a bit swifter, or I a little slower, I'd have had ample leisure to observe life in the Force from the inside—of the guardhouse. As I said, we went into the ante-room, and there I got my first peep at the divinity that doth hedge—not a king, but a commissioned officer in Her Majesty's N. W. M. P. An orderly held us up, and when MacRae had convinced him that our business was urgent, and not for his ears, he graciously allowed us to enter the Presence—who proved to be a heavy-set person with sandy, mutton-chop whiskers set bias on a vacuous, round, florid countenance. His braid-trimmed uniform was cut to fit him like the skin of an exceedingly well-stuffed sausage, and from his comfortable seat behind a flat-topped desk he gazed upon us with the wisdom of a tree-full of owls and the dignity of a stage emperor.

MacRae's heels clicked together and his right hand went up in the stiff military salute. The red-faced one acknowledged it by a barely perceptible flip of a fat paw, then put a little extra stiffening into his spinal column and growled, in a voice that seemed to come booming up from the region of his diaphragm, "Pro-ceed."

MacRae proceeded. But he didn't get very far. In fact, he'd barely articulated, 'I have to report, sir, that — — 'when the human sausage bethought himself of something more important, and held up one hand for silence. He produced a watch and studied it frowningly, then dismissed us and the recital of our troubles with a ponderous gesture.

"Repawt again," he rumbled, away down in his chest cavity, "at hawf—pawst—one."

"Yes, sir," MacRae saluted again, and we withdrew.

"A beautiful specimen; a man of great force," I unburdened myself when we got outside. "Have you many like him? I'd admire to see him cavorting around on the pinnacles after horse-thieves or whisky-runners or a bunch of bad Indians. A peaceable citizen would sure do well on the other side of the line if sheriffs and marshals took a lay-off to feed themselves when a man was in the middle of his complaint. How long do you suppose it will take that fat slob to get a squad of these soldier-policemen on the trail of that ten thousand?"

MacRae laughed dryly. "Old Dobson is harmless, all right, so far as hunting outlaws is concerned. But he doesn't cut much figure around here, one way or the other; no more than two or three other 'haw-haw' Englishmen who got commissions in the Force on the strength of their family connections. Lessard—the major in charge—is the brains of the post. He gets out and does things while these fatheads stay in quarters and untangle red tape. Personally, I don't like Lessard—he's a damned autocrat. But he's the man to whip this unorganized country into shape. I imagine he'll paw up the earth when he hears our story."

We mounted and rode to the stables. When we'd unsaddled and put up our horses, Mac led the way toward a row of small, whitewashed cabins set off by themselves, equidistant from barrack and officers' row.

"Sometimes I eat with the sergeants' mess," Mac said. "But generally I camp with 'Bat' Perkins when I drop in here. Bat's an ex-stock-hand like ourselves, and we'll be as welcome as payday. And he'll know if Lyn Rowan has come to Walsh."

I wasn't in shape, financially, to have any choice in the matter of a stopping-place. Forty or fifty dollars of expense money covered the loose cash in my pockets when I left Walsh for Benton; and, while I may have neglected to mention the fact, those two coin-collectors didn't overlook the small change when they held me up for La Pere's roll. There was a sort of sheebang—you couldn't call it a hotel if you had any regard for the truth—on the outskirts of Walsh, for the accommodation of wayfarers without a camp-outfit, but most of the time you couldn't get anything fit to eat there. So I was mighty glad to hear about Bat Perkins.

CHAPTER VII.

THIRTY DAYS IN IRONS!

It transpired, however, that before we reached Bat Perkins' cabin Mac got an unexpected answer to one of the questions he intended to ask. As we turned the corner of a rambling log house, which, from its pretentiousness, I judged must house some Mounted Police dignitary, we came face to face with a tall, keen-featured man in Police uniform, and a girl. Even though Rutter had declared she would be at Walsh, I wasn't prepared to believe it was Lyn Rowan. Sometimes five years will work a wonderful change in a woman; or is it that time and distance work some subtle transition in one's recollection? She didn't give me much time to indulge in guesswork, though. While I wondered, for an instant, if there could by any possibility be another woman on God's footstool with quite the same tilt to her head, the same heavy coils of tawny hair and unfathomable eyes that always met your own so frankly, she recognized the pair of us; though MacRae in uniform must have puzzled her for an instant.

"Gordon—and Sarge Flood! Where in the world did you come from? And—and——" She stopped rather suddenly, a bit embarrassed. I knew just as well as if she had spoken the words, that she had been on the point of asking him what he was doing in the yellow-striped breeches and scarlet jacket of a Mounted Policeman. Whatever had parted them, she hadn't held it against him. There was an indefinable something in the way she spoke his name and looked at him that told me there was still a soft spot in her heart for the high-headed beggar by my side.

But MacRae—while I was wise to the fact that he was the only friend I had in that country, and the sort of friend that sticks closer than a brother, I experienced a sincere desire to beat him over the noodle with my gun and thereby knock a little of the stiffness out of his neck—simply saluted the officer, tipped his hat to her, and passed on. I didn't *sabe* the play, and when I saw the red flash up into her face it made me hot, and there followed a few seconds when I took a very uncharitable view of Mr. Gordon MacRae's distant manner.

The fellow with her, I noticed, seemed to draw himself up very stiff and dignified when she stopped and spoke to us; and the look with which he favored MacRae was a peculiar one. It was simply a vagrant expression, but as it flitted over his face it lacked nothing in the way of surprised disapproval; I might go farther and say it was malignant—the kind of look that makes a man feel like reaching for a weapon. At least, that's the impression it made on me.

"I might fire that question back at you, Miss Rowan," I replied. "We're both a long way from the home range. I was here a day or two ago. How did you manage to keep out of sight—or have you just got in?"

"Yesterday, only," she returned. "We—you remember old Mammy Thomas, don't you?—came over from Benton with the Baker freight outfit. I expect to meet dad here, in a few days."

Her last sentence froze the words that were all ready to slip off the end of my tongue, and made my grouch against MacRae crystallize into a feeling akin to anger. Why couldn't the beggar stand his ground and deliver the ugly tidings himself? That bunch of cottonwoods with the new-made grave close by the dead horses seemed to rise up between us, and I became speechless. I hadn't the nerve to stand there and tell her she'd never see her father again this side of the pearly gates. Not I. That was a job for somebody who could put his arms around her and kiss the tears away from her eyes. Unless I read her wrong, there was only one man who could make it easier for her if he were by, and he was walking away as if it were none of his concern.

Something of this must have shown in my face, for she was beginning to regard me curiously. I gathered my scattered wits and started to make some attempt at conversation, but the man with the shoulder-straps forestalled me.

"Really, we must go, Miss Rowan, or we shall be late for luncheon," he drawled. The insolent tone of him was like having one's face slapped, and it didn't pass over Lyn's head by any means. I thought to myself that if he had set out to entrench himself in her good graces, he was taking the poorest of all methods to accomplish that desirable end.

"Just a moment, major," she said. "Are you going to be here any length of time, Sarge?"

"A day or so," I responded shortly. I didn't feel overly cheerful with all that bad news simmering in my brain-pan, and in addition I had conceived a full-grown dislike for the "major" and his I-am-superior-to-you attitude.

"Then come and see me this afternoon if you can. I'm staying with Mrs. Stone. Don't forget, now—I have a thousand things I want to talk about. Good-bye." And she smiled and turned away with the uniformed snob by her side.

MacRae had loitered purposely, and I overtook him in a few rods.

"Well," I blurted out, as near angry as I ever got at MacRae in all the years I'd known him, "you're a high-headed cuss, confound you! Is it a part of your new philosophy of life to turn your back on every one that you ever cared anything for?"

He shrugged his shoulders tolerantly. "What did you expect of me?"

"You might have—oh, well, I suppose you'll go your own gait, regardless," I sputtered. "That's your privilege. But I don't see how you had the nerve to pass *her* up that way. Especially since that Stony Crossing deal."

Mac took a dozen steps before he answered me.

"You don't understand the lay of things, Sarge," he said, rather hesitatingly. "If I have the situation sized up right, Lyn is practically alone here, and things are going to look pretty black to her when she learns what has happened. Hank never had anything much to do with his people. I doubt if Lyn has even a speaking acquaintance with her nearest kin. She has friends in the South—plenty of them who'd be more than glad to do as much for her as you or I. But we're a long way from the Canadian River, now. And so if she has made friends among the official set here, it's up to me to stand back—until that *cache* is found, anyway."

"Then you're not going to try and see her, and tell her about this thing yourself?" I asked.

"I can't," he replied impatiently. "You'll have to do that, Sarge. Hang it, can't you see where I stand? The mere fact that Lessard was taking her about shows that these officers' women have received her with open arms. They form a clique as exclusive as a quarantined smallpox patient, and a 'non-com' like myself is barred out, until I win a pair of shoulder-straps; when my rank would make me socially possible. Meantime, I'm a sergeant, and if Lyn went to picking friends out of the ranks, I'm not sure they wouldn't drop her like a hot potato. Sounds rotten, but that's their style; and you've been through the mill at home enough to know what it is to be knifed socially. It's different with you; you're an American citizen, a countryman of hers. You understand?"

"Yes," I answered tartly. "But I don't understand how you can stomach this sort of existence. What is there in it? Where is the profit or satisfaction in this kind of thing, for you? Will the man in the ranks get credit for taming the Northwest when his work is done? Why the devil don't you quit the job? Cut loose and be a free agent again."

"It is a temptation, the way things have come up in the last day or two," he mused. "I'd like to be foot-loose, so I could work it out without any string attached to me. But there are only two ways I could get out of the Force, and neither is open. I might desert, which would be a dirty way to sneak out of a thing I went into deliberately; or, if they were minded to allow me, I could buy my discharge—and

I haven't the price. Besides, I like the game and I don't know that I want to quit it. The life isn't so bad. It's your rabidly independent point of view. A man that can't obey orders is not likely to climb to a position where he can give them. What the dickens would become of the cow-outfits," he challenged, "if every stockhand refused to take orders from the foreman and owners? Do you stand on your dignity when La Pere tells you to do certain things in a certain way?"

I shrugged my shoulders. There was just enough truth in his words to make them hard to confute, and, anyway, I was not in the mood for that sort of argument. But I was very sure that I would rather be a forty-dollar-a-month cowpuncher than a sergeant in the Mounted Police.

"That fellow with her is the big gun here, is he?" I reverted to Lyn and her affairs.

"Yes," Mac answered shortly, "that was Lessard."

By this time we had come to the last cabin in the row. A whitewashed fence enclosed a diminutive yard, and as we turned in the gate Bat Perkins appeared in the doorway, both hands thrust deep in his trousers pockets and a pipe sagging down one corner of his wide mouth. He was rudely jovial in his greeting, as most of his type were. His wit was labored, but his welcome was none the less genuine.

"I seen yuh ride in, Mac," he grinned, "an' I told the old woman t' turn herself loose on the beefsteak an' spuds, for here comes that hungry-lookin' jasper from Pend d' Oreille."

I was duly made acquainted with Bat, and later with his wife, who, if she did have a trace of Indian blood in her, could certainly qualify as the patron saint of hungry men. Good cooks were a scarce article on the frontier then. Bat, I learned, was attached to the Force in a civilian capacity.

We ate, smoked a cigarette apiece, and then it was time for us to "repawt." So we betook ourselves to the seat of the mighty, to unload our troubles on the men who directed the destinies of the turbulent Northwest and see what they could do toward alleviating them.

This time the orderly passed us in without delay, and once more we faced the man of rank, who, after taking our measure with a deliberate stare, ordered MacRae to state his business.

As Mac related the unvarnished tale of the banked fire in the canyon, the hold-up, and the double murder, a slight sound caused me to turn my head, and I saw in a doorway that led to another room the erect figure of Major Lessard listening intently, a black frown on his eagle face. When MacRae had finished his story and the incapable blockhead behind the desk sat there regarding the two of us as though he considered that we had been the victims of a rank hallucination, Lessard slammed the door shut behind him and strode into the room.

"I'll take charge of this, Captain Dobson," he brusquely informed the red-faced numskull.

Taking his stand at the end of the desk, he made MacRae reiterate in detail the grim happenings of that night. That over, he quizzed me for a few minutes. Then he turned loose on MacRae with a battery of questions. Could he give a description of the men? Would he be able to identify them? Why did he not exercise more precaution when investigating anything so suspicious as a concealed fire? Why this, why that? Why didn't he send a trooper to report at once instead of wasting time in going to Stony Crossing? And a dozen more.

With every word his thin-lipped mouth drew into harder lines, and the cold, domineering tone, weighted heavy with sneering emphasis, grated on me till I wanted to reach over and slap his handsome, smooth-shaven face. But MacRae stood at "attention" and took his medicine dumbly. He had to. He was in the presence, and answering the catechism, of a superior officer, and his superior officer by virtue of a commission from the Canadian government could insult his manhood and lash him unmercifully with a viperish tongue, and if he dared to resent it by word or deed there was the guardhouse and the shame of irons—for discipline must be maintained at any cost! I thanked the star of destiny then and there that no Mounted Police officer had a string attached to me, by which he could force me to speak or be silent at his will. It was a dirty piece of business on Lessard's part. Even Dobson eyed him wonderingly.

"Why, damn it!" Lessard finally burst out, "you've handled this like a green one, fresh from over the water. You are held up; this man is robbed of ten thousand dollars; another man is murdered under your very nose—and then you waste thirty-six hours blundering around the country to satisfy your infernal curiosity. It's incredible, in a man of your frontier experience, under any hypothesis except that you stood in with the outlaws and held back to assure their escape!"

At first MacRae had looked puzzled, at a loss. Then under the lash of Lessard's bitter tongue the dull red stole up into his weather-browned cheeks, glowed there an instant and receded, leaving his face white under the tan. His left hand was at its old, familiar trick— fingers shut tight over the thumb till the cords stood tense between the knuckles and wrist—a never-failing sign that internally he was close to the boiling-point, no matter how calm he appeared on the surface. And when Lessard flung out that last unthinkable accusation, the explosion came.

"You lie, you— —!" MacRae spoke in a cold impersonal tone, and only the flat strained note betrayed his feeling; but the term applied to Lessard was one to make a man's ears burn; it was the range-riders' gauntlet thrown squarely in an enemy's face. "You lie when you say that, and you know you lie. I don't know your object, but I call your bluff—you—you blasted insect!"

Lessard, if he had been blind till then, saw what was patent to me— that he had gone a bit too far, that the man he had baited so savagely was primed to kill him if he made a crooked move. MacRae leaned forward, his gray eyes twin coals, the thumb of his right hand hooked suggestively in the cartridge-belt, close by the protruding handle of his six-shooter. They were a well-matched pair; iron-nerved, both of them, the sort of men to face sudden death open-eyed and unafraid.

A full minute they glared at each other across the desk corner. Then Lessard, without moving a muscle or altering his steady gaze, spoke to Dobson.

"Call the orderly," he said quietly.

Dobson, mouth agape, struck a little bell on the desk and the orderly stepped in from the outer room.

"Orderly, disarm Sergeant MacRae."

Lessard uttered the command evenly, without a jarring note, his tone almost a duplicate of MacRae's. He was a good judge of men, that eagle-faced major; he knew that the slightest move with hostile intent would mean a smoking gun. MacRae would have shot him dead in his tracks if he'd tried to reach a weapon. But a man who is really game—which no one who knew him could deny MacRae—won't, *can't* shoot down another unless that other shows *fight*; and a knowledge of that gun-fighters' trait saved Major Lessard's hide from being thoroughly punctured that day.

The orderly, a rather shaky orderly if the truth be told (I think he must have listened through the keyhole!) stepped up to Mac.

"Give me your side-arms, sergeant," he said, nervously.

MacRae looked from one to the other, and for a breath I was as nervous as the trooper. It was touch and go, just then, and if he'd gone the wrong way it's altogether likely that I'd have felt called upon to back his play, and there would have been a horrible mix-up in that two by four room. But he didn't. Just smiled, a sardonic sort of grimace, and unbuckled his belt and handed it over without a word. He'd begun to cool.

"Reduced to the ranks—thirty days in irons—solitary confinement!" Lessard snapped the words out with a wolfish satisfaction.

"Keep a close mouth, Sarge," MacRae spoke in Spanish with his eyes bent on the floor, "and don't quit the country till I get out." Then he turned at the orderly's command and marched out of the room.

When I again turned to Lessard he still stood at the end of the desk, industriously paring his fingernails. An amused smile wrinkled the corners of his mouth.

CHAPTER VIII.

LYN.

Whereas Lessard had acted the martinet with MacRae, he took another tack and became the very essence of affability toward me. (I'd have enjoyed punching his proud head, for all that; it was a dirty way to serve a man who had done his level best.)

"Rather unfortunate happening for you, Flood," he began. "I think, however, that we shall eventually get your money back."

"I hope so," I replied coolly. "But I must say that it begins to look like a big undertaking."

"Well, yes; it is," he observed. "Still, we have a pretty thorough system of keeping track of things like that. This is a big country, but you can count on the fingers of one hand the places where a man can spend money. Of course, you probably realize the difficulty of laying hands on men who know they are wanted, and act accordingly. We can't arrest on a description, because you wouldn't know the men if you saw them. Our only chance is to be on the lookout for free spenders. It's a certainty that they will be captured if they spend that money at any trading-post within our jurisdiction. I'll find out if the quartermaster knows the numbers and denomination of the bills. On the other hand, if they go south, cross the line, you know, we won't get much of a show at them. But we'll have to take chances on that."

"I've done all I can do in that direction," I said. "I've sent word to La Pere."

"You had better stay hereabout for a while," he decided. "You can put up at one of the troop-messes for a few days. I'll send a despatch to Whoop Up and MacLeod, and we'll see what turns up. Also I think I shall send a detail to bring in those bodies. The identification must be made complete. No doubt it will be a trial for Miss Rowan, but I think she would feel better to have her father buried here. By the way, you knew the Rowans in the States, I believe."

"Was trail-boss three seasons for Hank Rowan and his partner," I returned briefly. I didn't much like his offhand way of asking; not that it wasn't a perfectly legitimate query. But I couldn't get rid of the notion that he would hand me out the same dose he had given MacRae if only he had the power.

"Ah," he remarked. "Then perhaps you would like to go out and help bring in those bodies. It will save taking the Pend d' Oreille riders from their regular patrol, and we are having considerable trouble with whisky-runners these days."

I agreed to go, and that terminated the conversation. I didn't mind going; in fact some sort of action appealed to me just then. I had no idea of going back to Benton right away, and sitting around Fort Walsh waiting for something to turn up was not my taste. It never struck me till I was outside the office that Lessard had passed up the gold episode altogether; he hadn't said whether he would send any one to prognosticate around Writing-Stone or not. I wondered if he took any stock in Rutter's story, or thought it merely one of the queer turns a man's brain will sometimes take when he is dying. It had sounded off-color to me, at first; but I knew old Hans pretty well, and he always seemed to me a hard-headed, matter of fact sort of man, not at all the flighty kind of pilgrim that gets mixed in his mental processes when things go wrong. Besides, if there wasn't some powerful incentive, why that double killing, to say nothing of the incredible devilishness that accompanied it.

Once out of the official atmosphere, I hesitated over my next move. Lessard's high-handed squelching of MacRae had thrown everything out of focus. We'd planned to report at headquarters, see Lyn, if she were at Walsh, and then with Pend d' Oreille as a base of operations go on a still hunt for whatever the Writing-Stone might conceal. That scheme was knocked galley-west and crooked, for even when MacRae's term expired he'd get a long period of duty at the Fort; he'd lost his rank, and as a private his coming and going would be according to barrack-rule instead of the freedom allowed a sergeant in charge of an outpost like Pend d' Oreille—I knew that much of the Mounted Police style of doing business. And so far as my tackling single-handed a search for Hank Rowan's *cache*—well, I decided to see Lyn before I took that contract.

I hated that, too. It always went against my grain to be a bearer of ill tidings. I hate to make a woman cry, especially one I like. Some one had to tell her, though, and, much as I disliked the mission, I felt that I ought not to hang back and let some stranger blurt it out. So I nailed the first trooper I saw, and had him show me the domicile of Mrs. Stone—who, I learned, was the wife of Lessard's favorite captain—and thither I rambled, wishing mightily for a good stiff jolt out of the keg that Piegan Smith and Mac had clashed over. But if there was any bottled nerve-restorer around Fort Walsh it was tucked away in the officers' cellars, and not for the benefit of the common herd; so I had to fall back on a cigarette.

Lyn was sitting out in front when I reached the place. Another female person, whom I put down as Madam Stone, arose and disappeared through an open door at my approach. Lyn motioned me to a camp-stool close by. I sat down, and immediately my tongue became petrified. My think-machinery was running at a dizzy speed, but words—if silence is truly golden, I was the richest man in Fort Walsh that afternoon, for a few minutes, at least. And when my vocal organs did at last consent to fulfil their natural office, they refused to deliver anything but empty commonplaces, the kind one's tongue carries in stock for occasional moments of barren speech. These oral inanities only served to make Lyn give me the benefit of a look of amused wonder.

"Dear me," she laughed at last. "I wonder what weighty matter is crushing you to the earth. If you've got anything on your conscience, Sarge, for goodness' sake confess. I'll give you absolution, if you like, and then perhaps you'll be a little more cheerful."

"No, there's nothing particular weighing me down," I lied flatly. "Anyway, I don't aim to unload my personal troubles on you. I came over here to acquire a little information. How came you away up here by your lonesome, and what brought your father and old Hans— —"

Her purple-shaded eyes widened, each one a question-mark.

"Who told you that Hans was up North? I know I didn't mention him," she cut in quickly. "Have you seen them?"

It's a wonder my face didn't betray the fact that I was holding something back. I know I must have looked guilty for a second. That was a question I would gladly have passed up, but her eyes demanded an answer.

"Well," I protested, "it occurred to me that if you expected to meet your father here in a day or two, Rutter would naturally be with him, seeing that they've paddled in the same canoe since a good many years before you were born, my lady. What jarred you all loose from Texas? And what the mischief did you do to MacRae that he quit the South next spring after I did, and straightway went to soldiering in this country?"

She shied away from that query, just as I expected. "We had oceans of trouble after you left there, Sarge," she told me, turning her head from me so that her gaze wandered over the barrack-square. "It really doesn't make pleasant telling, but you'll understand better than some one that didn't know the country. You remember Dick Feltz, and that old trouble about the Conway brand that dad bought a long time back?"

I nodded; I remembered Mr. Feltz very well indeed, for the well-merited killing of one of his hired assassins was the main cause of my hasty departure from Texas.

"Well, it came to a head, one day, in Fort Worth. They shot each other up terribly, and a week or so later Feltz died. His people in the East got it into their heads that it was a case of murder. They stirred up the county authorities till every one was taking sides. Of course, dad was cleared; but that seemed to be the beginning of a steady run of bad luck. The trial cost an awful lot of money, and made enemies, too. Feltz had plenty of friends of his own calibre—you know that to your sorrow, don't you, Sarge?—and they started trouble on the range. It was simply terrible for a while. Dad can supply the details when he comes." ("when he comes"—I tell you, that jarred me.) "Finally things got to such a pass that dad had to quit. And what with a deal in some Mexican cattle that didn't turn out well, and some other business troubles that I never quite understood, we were just about finished when we closed out."

She let her eyes meet mine for an instant, and they were smiling, making light of it all. Most women, I thought, would have had a good cry, or at least pulled a long face, over a hard-luck story like that. But she was really more of a woman than I had thought her, and I thanked the Lord she was game when I remembered what I had to tell her before I was through.

"Dad and Hans Rutter, as you know, weren't the sort of men to sit around and mourn over anything like that," she laughed. "I don't know where they got the idea of going to Peace River. But dad settled me and Mammy Thomas in a little cottage in Austin, and they started. I wanted to go along, but dad wouldn't hear of it. They've been gone a little over two years. I'd get word from them about every three months, and early this spring dad wrote that they had made a good stake and were coming home. He said I could come as far as Benton to meet them, and we would take the boat from there down to St. Louis. So I looked up the lay of the country, and sent him word I would come as far as Walsh. He had said they would come out by way of this place. And then I rounded up Mammy Thomas and struck out. I've rather enjoyed the trip, too. They should be here any day, now."

My conscience importuned me to tell her bluntly that they would only come into Walsh feet first. But I dodged the unpleasant opening. There was another matter I wanted to touch upon first.

"Look here, Lyn," I said—rather dubiously, it must be confessed, for I didn't know how she would take it, "I'm going to tell you something on my own responsibility, and you mustn't get the idea that I'm trying to mix into your personal affairs without a warrant. But I have a hunch that you're laboring under a mistaken impression, right now; that is, if you care anything about an old friend like MacRae."

"I can't really say that I do, though," she assured me quickly, but she colored in a way that convinced me that her feeling toward MacRae was of the sort she would never admit to any one but himself.

"Well," I continued, "I imagined you would think it queer that he should pass you up as he did a while ago. But here at Fort Walsh we're among a class of people that are a heap different from Texas cow-punchers. These redcoats move along social lines that don't look like much to a cowman; but once in the Force you must abide by them. It was consideration for you that forbade MacRae to stop. Any woman in the company of an officer is taboo to an enlisted man, according——"

"I know all that," she interrupted impatiently. "Probably they'd cut me, and all that sort of thing. I understand their point of view, exactly, but I'm not here to play the social game, and I shall talk to whom it pleases me. Do you or Gordon MacRae honestly believe I care a snap for their petty conventions?"

"No, I know you better than that," I responded. "All the same, this is a pretty rough country for a woman, and if you've made friends among the people on top, they may come in handy. For that matter," I concluded, "you won't get a chance to have the cold shoulder turned to you for associating with MacRae; not for some time, anyway."

"What do you mean?" she demanded, in that answer-me-at-once way I knew of old.

"MacRae has gotten into a bad hole," I told her plainly. "Major Lessard, who happens to be the big chief in this neck of the woods, seems to have developed a sudden grouch against him. There was a hold-up night before last—in fact, I was the victim. I was separated from a big bunch of money that belongs to the outfit I'm working for. Mac was with me at the time. He had to come in here and report it, for it happened in his district, and the major raked him over the coals in a way that was hard to stand. You know MacRae, Lyn; it's mighty poor business for any man to tread on his toes, much less go walking rough-shod all over him. Lessard went the length of accusing him of being in with these hold-up men, because he did a little investigating on his own account before coming in to report. Mac took that pretty hard, and came mighty near making the major eat his words with gunpowder sauce on the side. So, for having the nerve to declare himself, he has lost his sergeant's stripes and has likewise gone to the guardhouse to meditate over the foolishness of taking issue with his superiors. If you don't see him for the next thirty days, you'll have the consolation of knowing that he isn't avoiding you purposely."

It was a rather flippant way to talk, but it was the best I could do under the circumstances. The last three days hadn't been exactly favorable to a normal state of mind, or well-considered speech.

But—who was the wise mortal that said: "No man knoweth the mind of a maid"?—she sat there quite unmoved, her hands resting quietly in her lap. "We all seem to be more or less under a cloud, Sarge," she said slowly. "Maybe when dad comes he can furnish a silver lining for it. I sometimes—what makes you look that way? You look as if you were thinking it my fault that Gordon is in trouble."

"You're wrong there," I protested, truthfully enough.

"But you have that air," she declared. "And I'm not to blame. If he hadn't been so—so—I'm sure he'd get out of the Mounted Police fast enough if he didn't like it. I can't imagine him doing anything against his will. I never knew him"—with a faint smile—"to stay anywhere or do anything that didn't suit him." She took to staring out across the grounds again, and one hand drew up slowly till it was doubled into a tight-shut little fist.

"Well, he's in that very fix right now. And he's likely to continue so, unless some one buys his release from the service and makes him a present of it. You might play the good angel," I suggested, half in earnest. "It only costs about five hundred dollars" — Mac had told me that — "and I'm sure he'd be properly grateful."

The red flag waved in her cheeks again. "I don't particularly like the idea," she said, rather crossly, still keeping her face turned away from me, "and I'm very sure he wouldn't care to have me. But dad thinks a lot of him; he might do something of the kind when he gets here. Dear, I wish they'd hurry along."

She had me at the end of my rope at last, and I felt like breaking away right there; any one not utterly calloused would, I think, have felt the same squeamishness with that sort of a tale crowding close. If she had been expecting bad news of any kind it wouldn't have been so hard to go on; but I couldn't beat about the bush any longer, so I made the plunge with what grace I could.

"Lyn, I've got something to tell you about your father and old Hans, and I'm afraid it's going to hurt," I prefaced gently, and went on before she could interrupt. "The fellows who held MacRae and me up had someway got wind of the gold they were packing out. They tried to get it. So far as I know, they haven't succeeded yet. Rutter tried to tell us where it was *cached*. There was a fight over it, you see, and he was shot. Mac and I came across him — but not soon enough." I stopped and got out cigarette material in an absent sort of way. My lips, I remember, were almighty dry just then.

"And dad?" Lyn was looking at me intently, and her voice was steady; that squeezed kind of steadiness that is almost worse than tears.

"He wasn't with Rutter." I drew a long breath and hurried on, slurring over the worst of it. "They had got separated. Hans was about done when we found him—he died in a few minutes—but he told us where to go. Then we went to look for your father. We found him; too late to do any good. We buried him—both of them—and came on here."

I felt like a beast, as if I had struck her with my fist, but at any rate, it was all told; all that she need ever know. I sat still and watched her, wondering nervously what she would do.

It was a strain to sit there silent, for Lyn neither did or said anything at first. Perhaps she cried afterward, when she got by herself, but not then; just looked at me, through me, almost, her face white and drawn into pained lines, and those purple-blue eyes perfectly black. I got up at last, and put one hand on her shoulder.

"It's hell, little girl, I know." I said this hardly realizing that I swore. "We can't bring the old man back to life, but we can surely run down the cold-blooded devils that killed him. I have a crow to pick with them myself; but that doesn't matter; I'd be in the game anyway. We'll get them somehow, when Mac gets out and can play his hand again. It was finding your father and giving him decent burial that kept us out so long. I don't understand, yet, why Lessard should pitch into MacRae so hard for doing that much. You know Mac, Lyn, and you know me—we'll do what we can."

She didn't move for a minute, and the shocked, stricken look in her eyes grew more intense. Then she dropped her head in the palms of her hands with a little sobbing cry. "Sarge, I—I wish you'd go, now," she whispered. "I want to—to be all by myself, for a while. I'll be all right by and by."

I stood irresolute for a second. It may have been my fancy, but I seemed to hear her whisper, "Oh, Gordon, Gordon!" Then I hesitated no longer, but turned away and left her alone with her grief; it was not for me to comfort her. And when I had walked a hundred yards or more, I looked back. She was still sitting as I had left her, head bowed on her hands, and the afternoon sun playing hide-and-seek in the heavy coils of her tawny-gold hair.

CHAPTER IX.

AN IDLE AFTERNOON.

For the next hour or two I poked aimlessly around the post buildings, chafing at the forced inaction and wondering what I would better do after I'd gone with the squad of redcoats to those graves and helped bring the bodies in. Even if I had a pack-horse and a grub-stake, it would be on a par with chasing a rainbow for me to start on a lone hunt for Hank Rowan's *cache*. I didn't know the Writing-Stone country, and a man had no business wandering up and down those somber ridges alone, away from the big freight-trails, unless he was anxious to be among the "reported missing" — which he sure would be if a bunch of non-treaty Indians ever got within gunshot of him. I damned Major Lessard earnestly for what I considered his injustice to MacRae, and wondered if he would send his troopers out to look for that hypothetical gold-dust. I didn't see how he could avoid making a bluff at doing so, even if he secretly classed Rutter's story as a fairy-tale, and I promised myself to find out what he was going to do before I started in the morning.

While I was sitting with my back against the shaded wall of troop G's barrack, turning this over in my mind, a Policeman with the insignia of a sergeant on his sleeve came sauntering leisurely by. He took me in with an appraising glance, and stopped.

"How d'ye do," he greeted, with a friendly nod. "You're the man that came in with MacRae, aren't you?"

I laconically admitted that I was.

"The k. o. has detailed me to bring in the bodies of the two men who were killed," he informed me. "He said that you were going along, and so I thought I'd hunt you up and tell you that we'll start about seven in the morning."

"I'll be ready," I assured him.

"Come on over to the bull-pen," he invited cordially. "Sorry we haven't a canteen in connection, but it's more comfortable over there. Good place to lop about, y' know; a decent place to sit, and a few books and cards and that sort of thing. Come along."

I rather liked the man's style, and as he seemed to be really anxious to make things pleasant for me, I shuffled off the pessimistic mood I was drifting into, and fell in with his proposal. The "bull-pen" proved to be a combination reading and lounging-room for the troopers not on duty. My self-appointed host, whose name was Goodell, waved me to a chair, and took one opposite. With his feet cocked up on a window-sill, and a cigarette going, he leaned back in his chair, and our conversation slackened so that I had a chance to observe my surroundings. It was a big place, probably fifty feet by a hundred, and quite a number of redcoats were sprinkled about, some reading, some writing letters, and two or three groups playing cards. None of them paid any attention to me, beyond an occasional disinterested glance, until my roving eyes reached a point directly behind me. Then I became aware that one of a bunch of four poker-players a few feet distant was regarding me with an expression that puzzled me. I had turned my head rather quickly and caught him staring straight at me. It was an odd look, sort of amused, and speculative; at least, that was the way I read it. Twice in the next ten minutes I glanced around quickly and caught him sizing me up, as it were; and then I hitched my chair sidewise, and deliberately began studying the gentleman to see if I could discover the source of his interest in me.

I failed in that, but I stopped his confounded quizzical stare. He wasn't the style of man that I'd care to stir up trouble with, judging from his size and the shape of his head. He was about my height, but half as broad again across the shoulders, and his thick, heavy-boned wrists showed hairy as an ape's when he stretched his arms to deal the cards. Aside from his physical proportions, there was nothing about the man to set him apart from his fellows. Half a dozen men in that room had the same shade of hair and mustache, and the same ordinary blue eyes. I turned back to the window again, thinking that

I was getting nervous as an old maid, to let a curious look from a stranger stir me like that.

In a few minutes the trooper opposite my friend of the poker-game drew out, and one of the players called loudly on Goodell to take his place. Goodell lighted another cigarette and nonchalantly seated himself in the vacant chair. Then I observed for the first time that the game was for blood rather than pastime, for Goodell paid for his little pile of white beans in good, gold coin of the realm. Next to playing a little "draw" myself, I like to watch the game, and so I moved over where I could see the bets made and the hands exhibited. And there I stuck till "stables" sounded, watching the affable sergeant outgeneral his opponents, and noting with some amusement the sulky look that grew more intensified on the heavy face of Hicks (as they called the man who had favored me with that peculiar stare) when Goodell finessed him out of two or three generous-sized pots.

On my way to attend to my horse, Bat Perkins overtook me.

"Say, old-timer, is it right about Mac losing his stripes and getting thirty days in the cooler?" he asked in lowered tone.

"It sure is," I answered emphatically.

"What in thunder for?" he inquired resentfully. And because I was aching to express my candid opinion of Major Lessard and all his works to some one who would understand my point of view, I told Bat all about it—omitting any mention of the gold-dust. Only four men, Dobson the fathead, Lessard, MacRae and myself, knew what little was known of that, and I felt that I had no license to spread the knowledge further.

"Oh, they sure do hand it to a man if he makes the least break," Bat sympathized. "Mac's one uh the best men they've got in the Force, an' they know it, too. Darned if that don't sound queer t' me; what else could he do? But Lessard's a overbearin' son-of-a-gun all round, and he's always breakin' out in a new place. Say, you might as well come over an' stay with me while you're round here. I don't reckon you'll enjoy herdin' with these rough-necks."

Bat's offer was not one to be overlooked by a man in my circumstances, so after supper found me sitting in his kitchen making gloomy forecasts of the future, between cigarettes. Shortly before the moon-faced clock nailed on the wall struck the hour of nine with a great internal whirring, some one tapped lightly on the door. Bat himself answered the knock. His body shut off sight of whoever stood outside. I could just catch the murmur of a subdued voice. After a few seconds of listening Bat nodded vigorously, and closed the door. He came back to his chair grinning pleasantly, and handed me a little package. I tore it open and found, wrapped tightly about three twenty-dollar gold pieces, an unsigned note from MacRae. It ran:

"Get after Lessard and see if he won't send an escort with you to Writing-Stone. If he does, and you find anything, I needn't warn you to be careful. I don't think he believed our yarn, at all. If he refuses to act, stay here till I get out. This money will hold you for a while. It's all I could rustle. If you need more, maybe Bat can stake you—he will if he can."

That was all. Not a word about Lyn. The stiff-necked devil!

"You know what this is, don't you?" I said to Bat. "How the dickens did he manage it?"

Bat's grin became even more expansive. "There ain't a buck trooper on the job," he replied, "that wouldn't help Mac if he got half a show; he's a white man. It's easy for a prisoner t' slip a note to a friend that happens t' be mountin' guard. He sent it t' me because I'd be apt t' know where yuh was. *Sabe?*"

I did. Mac's suggestion was right in line with my own idea. Lessard could scarcely refuse to do that much, I thought; and it would be rather unhealthy for those prairie pirates to match themselves against a bunch of Mounted Policemen who were on their guard—provided we found anything that was worth fighting over.

A little later Bat spread a bed for me on the kitchen floor, and I turned in. But my sleep resolved itself into a series of cat-naps. When the first sunbeam gleamed through the window of Bat's tiny kitchen, I arose, pulled on my boots and went to feed my horse. And when we had eaten breakfast I headed straight for Lessard's private quarters. I expected he would object to talking business out of business hours, but I didn't care; I wanted to know what he was going to do, before I started on that three-day trip. Fortunately Lessard was an early bird, like myself. I met him striding toward the building that seemed to be a clearing house for the official contingent.

"Good-morning, major," I said, mustering up a semblance of heartiness that was far from being the genuine article—I didn't like the man and it galled me to ask anything of him. "I want to ask you something before I leave. Have you talked this affair over with Miss Rowan?"

"Yes. Why?" He was maddeningly curt, but I pocketed my feelings and persisted.

"Then you must know beyond a doubt that there was some truth in Rutter's story," I declared. "Hank Rowan was my friend. I'd go out of my way any time to help his daughter. Will you send four or five of your men with me to the Writing-Stone to look for that stuff?" I asked him point-blank.

He looked me up and down curiously, and did not answer for a minute. "How do you know where to look?" he suddenly demanded. "Writing-Stone ridge is ten miles long. What chance would you have of finding anything in a territory of that extent?" His cold eyes rested on me in a disagreeable way. "I thought Rutter died before giving you the exact location."

As a matter of fact, MacRae, in detailing the lurid happenings of that night, did not repeat the words Rutter had gasped out with his last breath. He simply said that Hans died after telling us that they had been attacked, and that the gold was hidden at Writing-Stone. And Lessard, as I said before, had passed up the gold episode at the time; all his concern seemed to be for the robbers' apprehension, which was natural enough since a crime had undoubtedly been committed and he bore the responsibility of catching and punishing the perpetrators. The restoration of stolen goods was probably dwarfed in his mind by the importance of capturing the stealers.

I was vastly interested in that phase of it, too, for I realized that a speedy gathering in of those men of the mask was my only chance to lay hold of La Pere's ten thousand; and I had a theory that they were hardly the sort to be content with that sum, and that Hank Rowan's *cached* gold would be an excellent bait for them, if it could be uncovered. Those steadily reiterated phrases, "raw gold—on the rock" might have some understandable meaning if one were on the spot, but MacRae had kept that to himself—and I wasn't running a bureau of information for Lessard's benefit. The Canadian government might trust him, but I wouldn't—not if he took oath on a stack of Bibles, and gave a cast-iron bond to play fair. I couldn't give any sound reason for feeling that way, beyond the shabby treatment he'd given MacRae. But somehow the man's personality grated on me. Lessard was of the type, rare enough, that can't be overlooked if one comes in contact with it; a big, dominant, magnetic brute type that rouses either admiration or resentment in other ordinary mortals; the kind of a man that women become fascinated with, and other men invariably hate—and sometimes fear. I didn't stop to analyze my feeling toward him, just then; but I had the impulse to keep what little I knew to myself, and I obeyed the promptings of the sixth sense.

"He did," I answered. "But we can take a chance. Send men that know the country. Lyn Rowan's kinfolk are few and far between, now; that gold means a good deal to her, in her present circumstances."

"H—m-m." He mused a few seconds. Then: "If I think there's any possibility of finding it—well, I'll see what can be done, after those bodies are brought in. You, I suppose, are ready to start?"

I nodded.

"Sergeant Goodell is in charge of the detail. You'll probably find him about to go. That's all."

It was like being dismissed from parade; a right-about-face, march! command straight from the shoulder. Again I was overwhelmed with thankfulness that the N. W. M. P. had no string on me; I never took orders from anybody in that tone of voice, and I wanted to shake a defiant fist under the autocratic major's nose and tell him so. I had sense enough to see that the time and place was unpropitious for starting an argument of that sort, so I kept an unperturbed front and went about my business.

CHAPTER X.

THE VANISHING ACT, AND THE FRUITS THEREOF.

Being aware that it was near the time Goodell had named for starting, I returned to the stables, and, getting my horse, rode to the commissary. There I found Goodell engineering the final preparations. Four men, besides myself, made up the party: the sergeant, Hicks the hairy-wristed, another private, and a half-breed scout. They were lashing an allowance of food and blankets on a pack-horse, and two other horses with bare *aparejos* on their backs were tied to the horn of the breed's saddle—for what purpose I could easily guess.

While I sat on my *caballo* waiting for them to tie the last hitch a rattle of wheels and the thud of hoofs drew near, and presently a blue wagon, drawn by four big mules and flanked by half a dozen Mounted Policemen, passed by the commissary building. The little cavalcade struck a swinging trot as it cleared the barracks, swung down into the bed of Battle Creek, up the farther bank, and away to the west. And a little later we, too, left the post, following in the dusty wake of the paymaster's wagon and its mounted escort.

For ten or twelve miles we kept to the MacLeod trail at an easy pace, never more than a mile behind the "transient treasury," as Goodell facetiously termed it. He was a pretty bright sort, that same Goodell, quick-witted, nimble of tongue above the average Englishman. I don't know that he was English; for that matter, none of the three carried the stamp of his nationality on his face or in his speech. They were men of white blood, but they might have been English, Irish, Scotch or Dutch for all I could tell to the contrary. But each of them was broke to the frontier; that showed in the way they sat their horses, the way they bore themselves toward one another when clear of the post and its atmosphere of rigidly enforced discipline. The breed I didn't take much notice of at the time, except that when he spoke, which was seldom, he was given to using better language than lots of white men I have known.

At a point where the trail seemed to bear north a few degrees, Goodell angled away from the beaten track and headed straight across country for Pend d' Oreille. At noon we camped, and cooked a bite of dinner while the horses grazed; ate it, and went on again.

About three o'clock, as nearly as I could tell, we dipped into a wooded creek bottom some two hundred yards in width. The creek itself went brawling along in a deep-worn channel, and when my horse got knee deep in the water he promptly stopped and plunged his muzzle into the stream. I gave him slack rein, and let him drink his fill. The others kept on, climbed the short, steep bank, and passed from sight over its rim. I swung down from my horse on the brink of the creek, cinched the saddle afresh, and rolled a cigarette. If I thought about them getting the start of me at all, it was to reflect that they couldn't get a lead of more than two or three hundred yards, at the gait they traveled. Judge then of my surprise when I rode up out of the water-washed gully and found them nowhere in sight. I pulled up and glanced about, but the clumps of scrubby timber were just plentiful enough to cut off a clear view of the flat. So I fell back on the simple methods of the plainsman and Indian and jogged along on their trail.

Not for many days did I learn truly how I came to miss them, how and why they had vanished from the face of the earth so completely in the few minutes I lingered in the gulch. The print of steel-rimmed hoofs showed in the soft loam as plainly as a moccasin-track in virgin snow. Around a grove of quaking-aspens, eternally shivering in the deadest of calms, their trail led through the long grass that carpeted the bottom, and suddenly ended in a strip of gravelly land that ran out from the bed of the creek. I could follow it no farther. If there was other mark of their passing, it was hidden from me.

Wondering, and a bit exasperated, I spurred straight up the bank, and when I had reached the high benchland loped to a point that overlooked the little valley a full mile up and down. Cottonwood and willow, cut-bank and crooning water, lay green and brown and silver-white before, but no riders, no thing that moved in the shape of men came within the scope of my eyes. But I wasn't done yet. I turned away from the bank and raced up a long slope to a saw-backed ridge that promised largely of unobstructed view. Dirty gray lather stood out in spumy rolls around the edge of the saddle-blanket, and the wet flanks of my horse heaved like the shoulders of a sobbing woman when I checked him on top of a bald sandstone peak—and though as much of the Northwest as one man's eye may hope to cover lay bared on every hand, yet the quartet that rode with me from Fort Walsh occupied no part of the landscape. I could look away to the horizon in every direction, and, except for one little herd of buffalo feeding peacefully on the westward slant of the ridge, I could see nothing but rolling prairie, a vast undulating spread of grassland threaded here and there with darker lines that stood for creeks and coulées, and off to the north the blue bulk of the Cypress Hills.

I got off and sat me down upon a rock, rolled another cigarette, and waited. The way to Pend d' Oreille led over the ridge, a half mile on either side of me, as the spirit moved a traveler who followed an approximately straight line. Whatever road they had taken, they could not be more than three or four miles from that sentinel peak—for there is a well-defined limit to the distance a mounted man may cover in a given length of time. And from my roost I could note the passing of anything bigger than a buffalo yearling, within a radius of at least six miles. Therefore, I smoked my cigarette without misgiving, and kept close watch for bobbing black dots against the far-flung green.

I might as well have laid down and gone to sleep on that pinnacle for all the good my waiting and eye-straining did me. One hour slipped by and then another, and still I did not abandon hope of their appearance. Naturally, I argued with myself, they would turn back when I failed to overtake them—especially if they had thoughtlessly followed some depression in the prairie where I could not easily see them. And while I lingered, loath to believe that they were hammering unconcernedly on their way, the sun slid down its path in the western sky—slid down till its lower edge rested on the rim of the world and long black shadows began to creep mysteriously out of the low places, while buttes and ridges gleamed with cloth of gold, the benediction of a dying day. Only then did I own that by hook or by crook—and mostly by crook, I was forced to suspect—they had purposely given me the slip.

A seasoned cowpuncher hates to admit that any man, or bunch of men, can take him out into an open country and shake him off whenever it is desired; but if I had been a rank tenderfoot they couldn't have jarred me loose with greater ease. It was smooth work, and I couldn't guess the object, unless it was a Mounted Policeman's idea of an excellent practical joke on a supposedly capable citizen from over the line. Anyway, they had left me holding the sack in a mighty poor snipe country. Dark was close at hand, and I was a long way from shelter. So when the creeping shadows blanketed pinnacle and lowland alike, and all that remained of the sun was the flamboyant crimson-yellow on the gathering clouds, I was astride of my dun *caballo* and heading for Pend d' Oreille.

But speedily another unforeseen complication arose. Before I'd gone five miles the hoodoo that had been working overtime on my behalf got busy again. The clouds that were rolling up from the east at sundown piled thick and black overhead, and when dark was fairly upon me I was, for all practical purposes, like a blind man in an unfamiliar room. It didn't take me long to comprehend that I was merely wasting the strength of my horse in bootless wandering; with moonlight I could have made it, but in that murk I could not hope to find the post. So I had no choice but to make camp in the first coulée that offered, and an exceeding lean camp I found it—no grub, no fire, no rest, for though I hobbled my horse I didn't dare let his rope out of my hands.

About midnight the combination of sultry heat and banked clouds produced the usual results. Lightning first, lightning that ripped the sky open from top to bottom in great blazing slits, and thunder that cracked and boomed and rumbled in sharps and flats and naturals till a man could scarcely hear himself think; then rain in flat chunks, as if some malignant agency had yanked the bottom out of the sky and let the accumulated moisture of centuries drop on that particular portion of the Northwest. In fifteen minutes the only dry part of me was the crown of my head—thanks be to a good Stetson hat. And my arms ached from the strain of hanging onto my horse, for, hobbled as he was, he did his best to get up and quit Canada in a gallop when the fireworks began. To make it even more pleasant, when the clouds fell apart and the little stars came blinking out one by one, a chill wind whistled up on the heels of the storm, and I spent the rest of that night shivering forlornly in my clammy clothes.

Still a-shiver at dawn, I saddled up and loped for the crest of the nearest divide to get the benefit of the first sun-rays. But alas! the hoodoo was still plodding diligently on my trail. I topped a little rise, and almost rode plump into the hostile arms of a half-dozen breech-clout warriors coming up the other side. I think there were about half a dozen, but I wouldn't swear to it. I hadn't the time nor inclination to make an exact count. The general ensemble of war-paint and spotted ponies was enough for me; I didn't need to be told that it was my move. My spurs fairly lifted the dun horse, and we scuttled in the opposite direction like a scared antelope. The fact that the average Indian is not a master hand with a gun except at short range was my salvation. If they'd been white men I would probably have been curled in a neat heap within two hundred yards. As it was, they shot altogether too close for comfort, and the series of yells they turned loose in that peaceful atmosphere made me feel that I was due to be forcibly separated from the natural covering of my cranium if I lost any time in getting out of their sphere of influence.

The persistent beggars chased me a good ten miles before they drew up, concluding, I suppose, that I was too well mounted for them to overhaul. But it might have been a lot worse; I still had my scalp intact; the chase and its natural excitement had brought a comfortable warmth to my chilled body; and I had made good time in the direction I wished to go. On the whole, I felt that the red brother had done me rather a good turn. But I kept on high ground, thereafter, where I could see a mile or two, for I was very much alive to the fact that if another of those surprise-parties jumped me now that my horse was tired they would have a good deal of fun at my expense; and an Indian's idea of fun doesn't coincide with mine— not by a long shot!

I made some pointed remarks to my horse about Mr. Goodell and his companions, as I rode along. If Pend d' Oreille hadn't been the nearest place, I'd have turned back to Walsh and made that bunch of exhumers come back after me, if it were absolutely necessary that I should pilot them to the graves. Personally, I thought those two old plainsmen wouldn't thank Major Lessard or any one else for disturbing their last, long sleep; the wide, unpeopled prairies had always been their choice in life, and I felt that they would rather be laid away in some quiet coulée, than in any conventional "city of the dead" with prim headstones and iron fences to shut them in. A Western man likes lots of room; dead or alive, it irks him to be crowded.

I fully expected to find the four waiting for me at Pend d' Oreille, and I was prepared to hear a good deal of chaffing about getting lost. What of my waiting on the ridge that afternoon, and bearing more or less away from the proper direction at night, I did not reach the post till noon; and I was a bit puzzled to find only the men who were on duty there. I was digesting this along with the remains of the troopers' dinner, when Goodell and his satellites popped over the hill that looked down on Pend d' Oreille, and, a few minutes later, came riding nonchalantly up to the mess-house.

"Well, you beat us in," Goodell greeted airily. "Did you find a short cut?"

"Sure thing," I responded, with what irony I could command.

"Where the deuce *did* you go, anyway, after you stopped in that creek-bottom?" he asked, eying me with much curiosity. "We nearly played our horses out galloping around looking for you—after we'd gone a mile or so, and you didn't catch up."

"Then you must have kept damned close to the coulée-bottoms," I retorted ungraciously, "for I burnt the earth getting up on a pinnacle where you could see me, before you had time to go very far."

"Oh, well, it's easy to lose track of a lone man in a country as big as this," he returned suavely. "We all got here, so what's the odds? I guess we'll stick here till morning. We can't make the round trip this afternoon, and I'm not camping on the hills when it's avoidable."

It struck me that he was uncommonly philosophical about it, so I merely grunted and went on with my dinner.

That evening, when we went to the stable to fix up our horses for the night, I got a clearer insight into his reason for laying over that afternoon. They had been doing some tall riding, and their livestock was simply unfit to go farther. The four saddle-horses looked as if they had been dragged through a small-sized knothole; their gauntness, and the dispirited droop of their heads, spelled complete fatigue to any man who knew the symptoms of hard riding. By comparison, my sweat-grimed dun was fresh as a morning breeze.

CHAPTER XI.

THE GENTLEMAN WHO RODE IN THE LEAD.

It took us all of the next day to make the trip to Stony Crossing and back by way of the place where Rutter was buried. Goodell had no fancy, he said, for a night camp on the prairie when it could be avoided. He planned to make an early start from Pend d' Oreille, and thus reach Walsh by riding late the next night. So, well toward evening, we swung back to the river post. Goodell and his fellows were nowise troubled by the presence of dead men; they might have been packing so much merchandise, from their demeanor. But I was a long way from feeling cheerful. The ghastly burdens, borne none too willingly by the extra horses, put a damper on me, and I'm a pretty sanguine individual as a rule.

When we had unloaded the bodies from the uneasy horses, and laid them carefully in a lean-to at the stable-end, we led our mounts inside. Goodell paused in the doorway and emitted a whistle of surprise at sight of a horse in one of the stalls. I looked over his shoulder and recognized at a glance the rangy black MacRae had ridden.

"They must have given Mac's horse to another trooper," I hazarded.

"Not that you could notice," Goodell replied, going on in. "They don't switch mounts in the Force. If they have now, it's the first time to my knowledge. When a man's in clink, his nag gets nothing but mild exercise till his rightful rider gets out. And MacRae got thirty days. Well, we'll soon find out who rode him in."

I pulled the saddle off my horse, slapped it down on the dirt floor, and went stalking up to the long cabin. The first man my eyes lighted upon as I stepped inside was MacRae, humped disconsolately on the edge of a bunk. I was mighty glad to see him, but I hadn't time to more than say "hello" before Goodell and the others came in. Mac drew a letter from his pocket and handed it to Goodell.

He glanced quickly through it, then swept the rest of us with a quizzical smile. "By Jove! you must have a pull with the old man, Mac," he said to MacRae. "I suppose you know what's in this epistle?"

"Partly." Mac answered as though it were no particular concern of his.

"I'm to turn Hicks and Gregory over to you," he read the note again to be sure of his words, "see that you get a week's supply of grub here, and then leave you to your own devices. What's the excitement, now? Piegans on the war-path? Bull-train missing, or whisky-runners getting too fresh, or what? My word, the major has certainly established a precedent; you're the first man I've known that got thirty days in clink and didn't have to serve it to the last, least minute. How the deuce did you manage it? Put me on, like a good fellow—I might want to get a sentence suspended some day. Any of us are liable to get it, y'know." Goodell's tone was full of gentle raillery.

"The high and mighty sent me out to lead a forlorn hope," Mac dryly responded. "Does that look like a suspended sentence?" He turned his arm so that we could see the ripped stitching where his sergeant's stripes had been cut away.

"Tough—but most of us have been there, one time or another," Goodell observed sympathetically; and with that the subject rested.

Though I was burning to know things, we hadn't the least chance to talk that evening. Nine lusty-lunged adults in that one room prohibited confidential speech. Not till next morning, when we rode away from Pend d' Oreille with our backs to a sun that was lazily clearing the hill-tops, did MacRae and I have an opportunity to unburden our souls. When we were fairly under way in the direction of Writing-Stone, Hicks and Gregory—the breed scout—lagged fifty or sixty yards behind, and MacRae turned in his saddle and gave me a queer sort of look.

"I wasn't joking last night when I told Goodell that this was something of a forlorn hope," he said. "Are you ready to take a chance on getting your throat cut or being shot in the back, Sarge?"

I stared at him a second. It was certainly an astounding question, coming from that source—more like the language of the villain in a howling melodrama than a cold-blooded inquiry that called for a serious answer. But he was looking at me soberly enough; and he wasn't in the habit of saying startling things, unless there was a fairly solid basis of truth in them. He was the last man in the world to accuse of saying or doing anything merely for the sake of effect.

"That depends," I returned. "Why?"

"Because if we find what we're going after that's the sort of formation we may have to buck against until we get that stuff to Walsh," he replied coolly. "Beautiful prospect, eh? I reckon you'll understand better if I tell you how it came about.

"The day you left, Lessard had me up on the carpet again. When he got through cross-questioning me, he considered a while, and finally said that under the circumstances he felt that losing my stripes would be punishment enough for the rank insubordination I'd been guilty of, and he would therefore revoke the thirty-day sentence. I pricked up my ears at that, I can tell you, because Lessard isn't built that way at all. When a man talks to any officer the way I did to him, he gets all that's coming, and then some for good measure. I began to see light pretty quick, though. He went on to say that he had spoken to Miss Rowan about her father, and had learned that without doubt those two old fellows were headed this way with between forty and fifty thousand dollars in gold-dust, that they'd washed on Peace River. Since I'd been on the spot when Rutter died, and knew the Writing-Stone country so well, he thought I would stand a better show of finding their *cache* than any one else he could send out. He wanted to recover that stuff for Miss Rowan, if it were possible. So he wrote that order to Goodell and started me out to join you—with a warning to keep our eyes open, for undoubtedly the men who killed Rutter and held you up would be watching for a chance at us if we found that gold."

"Very acute reasoning on his part, I'm sure," I interrupted. "We knew that without his telling. And if he thinks those fellows are hanging about waiting for a whack at that dust, why doesn't he get out with a bunch of his troopers and round them up?"

"That's what," Mac grinned. "But wait a minute. This was about three in the afternoon, and he ordered me to start at once so as to catch you fellows as soon as possible. I started a few minutes after three. You remember the paymaster's train left that morning. He had a mounted escort of six or seven besides his teamster. The MacLeod trail runs less than twenty miles north of here, you know. I followed it, knowing about where they'd camp for the night, thinking I'd make their outfit and get something to eat and a chance to sleep an hour or two; then I could come on here early in the morning. I got to the place where I had figured they would stop, about eleven o'clock, but they had made better time than usual and gone farther, so I quit the trail and struck across the hills, for I didn't want to ride too far out of my way. When I got on top of the first divide I ran onto a little spring and stopped to water my horse and let him pick a bit of grass; I'd been riding eight hours, and still had quite a jaunt to make. I must have been about three miles south of the trail then."

He stopped to light the cigarette he had rolled while he talked, and I kept still, wondering what would come next. MacRae wasn't the man to go into detail like that unless he had something important to bring out.

"I sat there about an hour, I reckon," he continued. "By that time it was darker than a stack of black cats, and fixing to storm. I thought I might as well be moving as sit there and get soaked to the hide. While I was tinkering with the cinch I thought I heard a couple of shots. Of course, I craned my neck to listen, and in a second a regular fusillade broke out—away off, you know; about like a stick of dry wood crackling in the stove when you're outside the cabin. I loped out of the hollow by the spring and looked down toward the trail. The red flashes were breaking out like a bunch of firecrackers, and with pretty much the same sound. It didn't last long—a minute or so, maybe. I listened for a while, but there was nothing to be seen and I heard no more shooting. Now, I knew the pay-wagon was somewhere on that road, and it struck me that the bunch that got Hans and Rowan and held us up might have tried the same game on it; and from the noise I judged it hadn't been a walkaway. It was a wild guess; but I thought I ought to go down and see, anyway. Single-handed, and in that dark you could almost feel, I knew I was able to sidestep the trouble, if it should be Indians or anything I didn't care to get mixed up in.

"I'd gone about a mile down the slope when the lightning began to tear the sky open. In five minutes the worst of it was right over me, and one flash came on top of the other so fast it was like a big eye winking through the clouds. One second the hills and coulées would show plain as day, and next you'd have to feel to find the ears of your horse. I pulled up, for I didn't care to go down there with all that lightning-play to make a shining mark of me, and while I sat there wondering how long it was going to last, a long, sizzling streak went zig-zagging up out of the north and another out of the east, and when they met overhead and the white glare spread over the clouds, it was like the sun breaking out over the whole country. It lit up every ridge and hollow for two or three seconds, and showed me four riders tearing up the slope at a high run. I don't think they saw me at all, for they passed me, in the dark that shut down after that flash of lightning, so close that I could hear the pat-a-pat of the hoofs. And when the next flash came they were out of sight.

"Right after that the rain hit me like a cloudburst. That was over quick, and by the time it had settled to a drizzle I was down in the paymaster's camp. Things were sure in an uproar there. Two men killed, two more crippled, and the paymaster raving like a maniac. I hadn't been far wide of the mark. The men that passed me on the ridge had held up the outfit—and looted fifty thousand dollars in cold cash."

"Fifty thousand—the devil!" I broke in. "And they got away with it?"

"With all the ease in the world," MacRae answered calmly. "They made a sneak on the camp in the dark, clubbed both sentries, and had their guns on the rest before they knew what was wrong. They got the money, and every horse in camp. The shooting I heard came off as they started away with the plunder. Some of the troopers grabbed up their guns and cut loose at random, and these hold-up people returned the compliment with deadly effect.

"That isn't all," he continued moodily. "I stayed there till daylight, and then gathered up their stock. All the thieves wanted of the horses was to set the outfit afoot for the time being—a trick which bears the earmarks of the bunch that got in their work on us. They had turned the horses loose a mile or so away, and I found them grazing together. When I'd brought them in I got a bite to eat and came on about my own business.

"Up on the ridge, close by the spring I had stopped at, I came slap on their track; the four horses had pounded a trail in the wet sod that a kid could follow. I tore back to the paymaster's camp and begged him to get his men mounted and we would follow it up. But he wouldn't listen to such a thing. I don't know why, unless he had some money they had overlooked and was afraid they might come back for another try at him. So I went back and hit the trail alone. It led south for a while, and then east to Sage Creek. This was day before yesterday, you *sabe*. Near noon I found a place where they'd *cached* two extra horses in the brush on Sage Creek. After that their track turned straight west again, and it was hard to follow, for the ground was drying fast. Finally I had to quit—couldn't make out hoof-marks any more. And it was so late I had to lie out that night. I got to Pend d' Oreille yesterday morning two or three hours after you fellows left for the crossing."

I haven't quite got a gambler's faith in a hunch, or presentiment, or intuitive conclusion—whatever term one chooses to apply—but from the moment he spoke of seeing four riders on a ridge during that frolic of the elements, a crazy idea kept persistently turning over and over in my mind; and when Mac got that far I blurted it out for what it was worth, prefacing it with the happenings of the trip from Walsh to Pend d' Oreille. He listened without manifesting the interest I looked for, tapping idly on the saddle-horn, and staring straight ahead with an odd pucker about his mouth.

"I was just going to ask you if you all came through together," he observed, in a casual tone. "I neglected to say that I got a pretty fair look at those fellows. In fact, I wouldn't hesitate to swear to the face of the gentleman who rode in the lead of the four."

"You did? Was it—was my hunch right?" I demanded eagerly.

"I could turn in my saddle and shoot his eye out," MacRae responded whimsically. "And I don't know but that would be more than justice. Of course, the others were the men, but I'm positive of Gregory. You see what we're up against, Sarge.

"That's why," he soberly concluded, "I think we'll have our hands full if we do locate that stuff. It's a big chunk of money, and a little thing like killing a man or two won't trouble them. We'll be watched every minute of the time that we prowl around those painted rocks; that's a cinch. And when we've pulled the chestnut out of the fire they'll gobble it—if there's the ghost of a chance."

While I was digesting this unpalatable information, Hicks and Gregory spurred abreast of us; for the remainder of the journey we four rode elbow to elbow, and conversation was scant.

Mid-afternoon found us camped under the Stone. Once on the ground, I began to think we were in no immediate danger of getting our throats cut for the sake of the treasure. Rutter had said "under the Stone"—and the vagueness of his words came home to me with considerable force, for the Stone, roughly estimated, was a good mile in length. It paralleled the river, a perpendicular wall of gray sandstone. An aptly-named place; wherever a ledge offered foothold, and even in places that seemed wholly beyond reach of human hands, the bald front of the cliff was chiseled with rude traceries—the picture-writing of the Blackfoot tribe. The history of a thousand battles and buffalo-hunts was written there. And somewhere at the foot of that mile-long cliff, under the uncouth figures carved by the red men in their hour of triumphant ease, rested that which we had come to find. I sat with my back against a cottonwood and smoked a cigarette while I considered the impassive front of Writing-On-the-Stone; and the fruit of my consideration was that he who sought for the needle in the haystack had no more difficult task than ours.

In due time we ate supper, and dark spread its mantle over the land. Then MacRae and I crawled up on a projecting ledge of rock to roll out our blankets—in a place where we could not well be surprised. Not that either of us anticipated anything of the sort so early in the game; when we had found what we were after, that would come. But the mere fact that we were all playing a part made us incline to caution. I don't know if we betrayed our knowledge or suspicions to Hicks and Gregory, but it was a good deal of an effort to treat those red-handed scoundrels as if they were legitimate partners in a risky enterprise. We had to do it, though. Until they showed their hand we could do nothing but stand pat and wait for developments; and if they watched us unobtrusively, we did the same by them. It is not exactly soothing to the nerves, however, to be in touch all day and then lie down to sleep at night within a few feet of men whom you imagine are only awaiting the proper moment to introduce a chunk of lead into your system or slip a knife under your fifth rib. I can't truthfully say that I slept soundly on that ledge.

CHAPTER XII.

WE LOSE AGAIN.

Three days later MacRae and I scaled the steep bank at the west end of the cliff and threw ourselves, panting, on the level that ran up to the sheer drop-off. When we had regained the breath we'd lost on that Mansard-roof climb we drew near to the edge, where we could stare into the valley three hundred feet below while we made us a cigarette apiece. We were just a mite discouraged. Beginning that first morning at the east end of the Writing-Stone we had worked west, conning the weather-worn face of it for a mark that would give a clue to the *cache*. Also we had scanned carefully the sandy soil patches along the boulder-strewn base, seeking the tell-tale footprints of horse or man. And we had found nothing. Each day the conviction grew stronger upon us that finding that gold would be purely chance, a miracle of luck; systematic search had so far resulted in nothing but blistered heels from much walking. And unless we did find it, thereby giving the gentlemen of the mask some incentive to match themselves against us once more, we were not likely to have the opportunity of breaking up a nervy bunch of murdering thieves.

We reasoned that the men whose guns we had looked into over Rutter's body and those who robbed the paymaster on the MacLeod trail were tarred with the same stick; likewise, that even now two of them ate out of the same pot with us three times daily. The thing was to prove it. Personally, the paymaster's trouble was none of my concern; what I wanted was to get back that ten thousand dollars, or deal those hounds ten thousand dollars' worth of misery. Not that I wasn't willing to take a long chance to help Lyn to her own, but I was human enough to remember that I had a good deal at stake myself. It was a rather depressed stock-hand, name of Flood, who blew cigarette smoke out over the brow of Writing-Stone that evening.

74

Mac finished smoking and ground the stub into the earth with his heel. For another minute or two he sat there without speaking, absently flipping pebbles over the bank.

"I reckon we might as well poke along the top to camp," he said at last, getting to his feet. "I sent that breed back, down there, so we could talk without having to keep cases on him. This is beginning to look like a hopeless case, isn't it?"

"Somewhat," I admitted. "I did think that Rutter's description would put us on the right track when we got there; but I can't see much meaning in it now. I suppose we'll just have to keep on going it blind."

"We'll have to stay with it while there's any chance," he said thoughtfully. "But I've been thinking that it might be a good plan to take a fall out of those two." He jerked his thumb in the direction of camp. "If we have sized things up right, they'll make some sort of move, and if we're mistaken there will be no harm done. I'll tell you an idea that popped into my head a minute ago. We can pretend to locate the stuff. Fix up a couple of dummy sacks, you know, and get them to camp and packed on the horse without letting them see what's inside. If Lyn gave Lessard the right figures, there should be between a hundred and forty or fifty pounds of dust. It's small in bulk, but weighty as a bad conscience. If we had a couple of little sacks we could get around that problem, easy enough—this black sand along the river would pass for gold-dust in weight. We could make the proper sort of play, and give them the chance they're looking for. If they make a break it'll be up to us to get the best of the trouble."

"It might work," I replied. "If you think it would make them tip their hand, I'm with you. This watch-the-other-fellow business is making me nervous as an old woman. Once we had those two dead to rights they might let out something that would enable us to land the whole bunch, and the plunder besides; once we had them rounded up we could come back here and hunt for Hank Rowan's gold-dust in peace."

"You've got the idea exactly, and we'll see what we can do in the morning," Mac returned. "But don't get married to the notion that they'll cough up all they know, right off the reel. Hicks might, if you went at him hard enough. But not the other fellow. Gregory's game clear through—he's demonstrated that in different ways since I've been in the Force. You could carve him to pieces without hearing a cheep, if he decided to keep his mouth shut. And he's about as dangerous a man in a scrimmage as I know. If there's a row, don't overlook Mr. Gregory."

We hoofed it toward camp as briskly as our galled feet would permit, for the sun was getting close to the sky line, and talked over Mac's scheme as we went. There was no danger of being overheard on that bench. As a matter of fact, Hicks and Gregory didn't know we were up there; at least, they were not supposed to know. MacRae had made a practice of leaving one or the other in camp, in case some prowling Indians should spy our horses and attempt to run them off. That afternoon Hicks had been on guard. When Mac started Gregory back he told him that we would be along presently, then sat himself down on a rock and watched the breed. When he was far enough up the flat to lose track of our movements we dropped into a convenient washout and sneaked along it to the foot of the bank, where a jutting point of rock hid sight of us climbing the hill.

We had no thought of spying on them, at first—it was simply to be rid of their onerous presence for a while, and getting on the bench was an afterthought. But as we came opposite camp, MacRae took a notion to look down and see what they were about. At a point which overlooked the bottom some two hundred yards from the east end of the Stone, we got down on our stomachs and wriggled carefully to the naked rim of the cliff. For some time we laid there, peering down at the men below. Hicks was puttering around the fire, evidently cooking supper, and Gregory was moving the picket rope of his horse to fresh grass. There was nothing out of the ordinary to be seen, and I drew back. But MacRae still kept his place. When he did back away from the edge, he had the look of a man who has made some important discovery.

"On my soul, I believe I've found it," he calmly announced.

"What!"

"I believe I have," he repeated, a trace of exultation in his tone. "At least, it amounts to the same thing. Crawl up there again, Sarge, and look straight down at the first ledge from the bottom. Hurry; you won't see anything if the sun has left it. And be careful how you show your head. We don't want to get them stirred up till we have to."

Cautiously I peeped over the brink, straight down as Mac had directed. The shadow that follows on the heels of a setting sun was just creeping over the ledge, but the slanting rays lingered long enough to give me sight of a glittering patch on the gray stone shelf below. While I stared the sun withdrew its fading beams from the whole face of the cliff, but even in the duller light a glint of yellow showed dimly, a pin point of gold in the deepening shadow.

Gold! I drew back from the rim of Writing-On-the-Stone, that set of whispered phrases echoing in my ears. Mac caught my eye and grinned. "*Gold—raw gold—on the rock—above.*" I mouthed the words parrotlike, and he nodded comprehendingly.

"Oh, thunder!" I exclaimed. "Do you reckon *that's* what he meant?"

"What else?" Mac reasoned. "They'd mark the place somehow—and aren't those his exact words? What dummies we were not to look on those ledges before. You can't see the surface of them from the flat; and we might have known they would hardly put a mark where it could be seen by any pilgrim who happened to ride through that bottom."

"Hope you're right," I grunted optimistically.

"We'll know beyond a doubt, in the morning," Mac declared. "To-night we won't do anything but eat, drink, and sleep as sound as possible, for to-morrow we may have one hell of a time. I prefer to have a few hours of daylight ahead of us when we raise that *cache*. Things are apt to tighten, and I don't like a rumpus in the dark. Just now I'm hungry. If that stuff is there, it will keep. Come on to camp; our troubles are either nearly over or just about to begin in earnest."

We followed the upland past the end of the Stone till we found a slope that didn't require wings for descent. If Hicks or Gregory wondered at our arrival from the opposite direction in which we should have appeared, they didn't betray any unseemly curiosity. Supper and a cigarette or two consumed the twilight hour, and when dark shut down we took to our blankets and dozed through the night.

At daybreak we breakfasted. Without a word to any one MacRae picked up his carbine and walked out of camp. I followed, equally silent. It was barely a hundred yards to the ledge, and I caught myself wishing it were a good deal farther—out of range of those watchful eyes. I couldn't help wondering how it would feel to be potted at the moment of discovery.

"I thought I'd leave them both behind, and let them take it out in guessing," Mac explained, when we stood under the rock shelf upon which we had looked down the evening before. "We're right under their noses, so they won't do anything till the stuff's actually in sight."

He studied the face of the cliff for a minute. The ledge jutted out from the towering wall approximately twenty feet above our heads, but it could be reached by a series of jagged points and knobs; a sort of natural stairway—though some of the steps were a long way apart. Boulders of all shapes and sizes lay bedded in the soft earth where we stood.

"You shin up there, Sarge," Mac commanded, "and locate that mark. It ought to be an easy climb."

I "shinned," and reached the ledge with a good deal of skin peeled from various parts of my person. The first object my eye fell upon as

I hoisted myself above the four-foot shelf was a dull, yellow spot on the gray rock, near enough so that I could lean forward and touch it with my fingers. A two-inch circle of the real thing—I'd seen enough gold in the raw to know it without any acid test—hammered into the coarse sandstone. I pried it up with the blade of my knife and looked it over. Originally it had been a fair-sized nugget. Hans or Rowan had pounded it into place with the back of a hatchet (the corner-marks told me that), flattening it to several times its natural diameter. I threw it down to MacRae, and looked carefully along the ledge. There was no other mark that I could see; I began to wonder if we were as hot on the scent as we had thought.

"Is there a loose piece of rock up there?" Mac called presently. "If there is, set it on the edge, in line with where this was."

I found a fragment about the size of my fist and set it on the rim of the ledge. He squinted up at it a moment, then nodded, smiling.

"Come on down now, Sarge," he grinned; and, seating himself on a rock with the carbine across his knees, he began to roll a cigarette, as if the finding of Hank Rowan's gold-*cache* were a thing of no importance whatever.

"Well," I began, when I had negotiated that precarious succession of knobs and notches and accumulated a fresh set of bruises, "why don't you get busy? How much wiser are you now? Where's your gold-dust?"

He took a deliberate puff and squinted up at the ledge again. "I'm sitting on it, as near as I can figure," he coolly asserted.

"Yes, you are," I fleered. "I'm from Missouri!"

"Oh, you're a doubting Thomas of the first water," he said. "Stand behind me, you confounded unbeliever. Kink your back a little and look over that stone you set for a mark. Do you see anything that catches your attention?"

Getting in the position he suggested, I looked up. Away back in the days before the white man was a power to be reckoned with in the Indian's scheme of things, some warrior had stood upon that self-same ledge and hacked out with a flint chisel what he and his fellows doubtless considered a work of art. Uncanny-looking animals, and uncannier figures that might have passed for anything from an articulated skeleton to a Missing Link, cavorted in a long line across that tribal picture-gallery. Between each group of figures the face of the rock was scored with mysterious signs and rudely limned weapons of war and chase. Right over the stone marker, a long-shafted war-lance was carved—the blade pointing down. MacRae's seat, stone-marker, and aboriginal spearhead; the three lined up like the sights of a modern rifle. The conclusion, in the light of what we knew from Rutter, was obvious, even to a lunkhead like myself.

"It looks like you might have struck it," I was constrained to admit.

Mac threw away his cigarette. "Here and now is where we find out," he declared.

Worming our fingers under the edge of the boulder, we lifted with all the strength that was in us. For a second it seemed that we could never budge it. Then it began to rise slowly, so slowly that I thought the muscles of my back would snap, and MacRae's face close by mine grew red and then purple with the strain. But it moved, and presently a great heave turned it over. Bedded in the soft earth underneath lay the slim buckskin sacks. Our fingers, I remember, trembled a bit as we stood one on end and loosened its mouth to make sure if we had found the treasure for which two men had already lost their lives.

"Here"—Mac handed me his carbine—"you stay with the yellow temptation. From now on we'll have to keep a close eye on this stuff, and likewise have our guns handy. I'll make those fellows pack up and bring the horses here. Then we'll load this and pull for Walsh."

BEDDED IN THE SOFT EARTH UNDERNEATH LAY THE SLIM
BUCKSKIN SACKS.

His first move was to saddle his black horse and my dun. These he led to the fire, and thereafter stood a little to one side, placidly consuming a cigarette while the other two packed the camp-outfit and saddled their own mounts. Then they trailed across the flat toward me, MacRae blandly bringing up the rear. He wasn't taking any chances.

Half an hour later, with the sacks of gold securely lashed on the *aparejos* of the pack-horse, we climbed out of Writing-Stone bottom and swung away over the silent tablelands.

With Writing-on-the-Stone scarcely three miles behind, the long-abandoned burrow of a badger betrayed us into the hands of the enemy. (What a power for thwarting the plans of men little things sometimes exercise!) We had contrived that Gregory should lead the pack-horse, which gave MacRae and me both hands to use in case of a hostile demonstration; that there would be such, neither of us doubted from the moment those two laid eyes on the buckskin sacks. The sidelong, covetous glance that passed between them bespoke what was in their minds. And from that time on the four of us were like so many open-headed casks of powder sitting by a fire; sooner or later a spark would bring the explosion. We had them at a disadvantage trotting across the level upland, Gregory in the lead and Hicks sandwiched between Mac and myself—until MacRae's horse planted his foreleg to the knee in an old badger-hole hidden under a rank accumulation of grass. The black pitched forward so suddenly that Mac had no time to swing clear, and as he went down under the horse Gregory's agile brain grasped the opportunity of the situation, and his gun flashed out of its scabbard.

My hand flew to mine as I jerked the dun up short, but I wasn't fast enough—and Hicks was too close. It was a trilogy of gun-drawing. Gregory drew his and fired at MacRae with the devilish quickness of a striking rattler; I drew with intent to get Mr. Gregory; and Hicks drew his and slapped me over the head with it, even as my finger curled on the trigger. My gun went off, I know—afterward I had a dim recollection of a faint report—but whether the bullet went whistling into the blue above or buried itself in the broad bosom of the Territory, I can't say. Things ceased to happen, right then and there, so far as I was concerned. And I haven't satisfied myself yet why Hicks struck instead of shooting; unless he had learned the frontier lesson that a bullet in a vital spot doesn't *always* incapacitate a man for deadly gun-play, while a hard rap on the head invariably does. It wasn't any scruple of mercy, for Hicks was as cold-blooded a brute as ever glanced down a gun-barrel.

When my powers of sight and speech and hearing returned, MacRae stood over me, nowise harmed. The black horse lay where he had fallen. I sat up and glanced about, thankful that I was still in the flesh, but in a savage mood for all that. This, thought I, is a dismal-looking outcome—two men and a dead horse left high and dry on the sun-flooded prairie. And a rampant ache in my head, seconded by a medium-sized gash in the scalp, didn't make for an access of optimism at that moment.

"Well," I burst out profanely, "we lose again, eh?"

"Looks like it," Mac answered laconically. Then he whirled about and walked to a little point some distance away, where he stood with his back to me, looking toward Lost River.

CHAPTER XIII.

OUTLAWED.

I sat where I was for a while, fingering my sore head and keeping my thoughts to myself, for I had a keen sense of the mood he was in. For the second time, through no fault of his own, he had failed to live up to that tradition of the Force which accepts nothing short of unqualified victory for a Mounted Policeman when he clashes with breakers of the law. And, in addition, he had let slip through his fingers a fortune that belonged to a woman for whom he cared a great deal more than he was willing to admit. I felt pretty small and ashamed myself, to think of the ease with which they had left us afoot on the bald prairie after all our scheming, our precaution against something we were sure would happen; and there was no responsibility on my shoulders—except for that ten thousand of La Pere's, which I was beginning to think I'd looked my last upon. Mac had not only the knowledge of personal failure—bitter enough, itself, to a man of his temperament—to gnaw at him, but the prospect of another grilling from the powers in gold braid. It would have been strange if he hadn't felt blue.

He came back, however, in a few minutes, and squatting beside me abstractedly got out papers and tobacco.

"I suppose that bunch will quit the country now," he remarked at length. "They've got their hands on a heap of money in the last ten days; all they'll have a chance to grab for some time. And they've come out into the open. So there's not much doubt of their next move—they'll be on the wing."

"Well, we have a cinch on identifying them now," I commented. "We've got that much out of the deal. If the Mounted Police are half as good man-hunters as they are said to be, they ought to round up that bunch in short order. Did the black hurt you when he fell?"

"Bruised my leg some," he returned indifferently. Then, scowling at the remembrance: "If he hadn't caught me right under him I'd have got action on those two. But the jar threw my six-shooter where I couldn't reach it, and the carbine was jammed in the stirrup-leather on the wrong side. I reckon Gregory thought he got me first shot. He would have, too, only Crow threw up his head and stopped the bullet instead of me. They had ducked into that coulée by the time I got clear. Hicks grabbed your horse and took him along. I'm somewhat puzzled to know why they didn't stand pat and make a clean job of us both. Blast them, anyway!"

"Same here, and more of it," I fervently exclaimed.

"Come on, let's get out of here," Mac abruptly proposed. "We'll have to make Pend d' Oreille and send word to Walsh. It'll take the whole force to catch them now."

My gun lay where it had fallen when Hicks whacked me over the head. I picked it up, replaced the empty cartridge, and shoved it back into the scabbard. MacRae hoisted the carbine to his shoulder, and we started.

We poked along slowly at first, for I was still a bit dizzy from that blow. Before long we came to a spring seeping from the hillside, and when I had bathed my head in the cool water I began to feel more like myself. Thereafter, we tramped silently across high, dry benches, slid and scrambled to the bottoms of an endless succession of coulées, and wearily climbed the steep banks that lay beyond. The cool morning wind died away; the sun reeled up on its appointed circle, glaring brazenly into every nook and cranny in the land. Underfoot, the dry sod grew warm, then hot, till the soles of our boots became instruments of torture to feet that were sadly galled by fruitless tramping around the Stone. When a man has grown up in the habit of mounting a horse to travel any distance over three hundred yards, a walk of twenty undulating miles over a network of bald ridges and yawning coulées makes him think that a sulphur-and-brimstone hereafter can't possibly hold much discomfort that he hasn't sampled. A cowpuncher in high-heeled riding-boots is handicapped for pedestrianism by both training and inclination—and that scarred and wrinkled portion of the Northwest is a mighty poor strolling-ground for any man.

But we kept on, for the simple reason that there was nothing else we could do. MacRae wasted no breath in words. If the heat and the ungodly steepness of the hills and the luke-warm water that trickled along the creek channels ruffled his temper, he made no noise about it, only pressed doggedly toward Pend d' Oreille. I daresay he thought I was attending to that part of it, registering a complaint for both of us. And if I didn't rise to the occasion it was the fault of my limited vocabulary. I kept a stiff backbone for a while, but presently a futile rage against circumstances bubbled up and boiled over. I climbed each succeeding canyon wall oozing perspiration and profanity, and when the top was reached took fresh breath and damned the Northwest by sections in a large, fluent manner of speech. In time, however, the foolishness of this came home to me, and I subsided into spasmodic growling, saving my wind for the miles yet to cover.

Well past noon we reached the summit of a hog-backed ridge that overlooked the tortuous windings of Lost River, a waterless channel between banks that were void of vegetation. The crest of the divide was studded with great outcroppings of sand-stone, and in the shadow of one giant rock we laid down to rest before we descended into that barren valley where the heat-waves shimmered like crepon silk. The cool bit of earth was good to stretch upon; for nearly an hour we laid there, beyond reach of the glowing sun; it was worth almost the treasure we had lost to ease our aching feet. Then reluctantly we started again.

As we stepped from behind the rock three riders came into sight on the opposite slope of Lost River. A moment's scrutiny assured us that they were Mounted Policemen. From habit our eyes swept the surrounding country, and in a moment we observed other groups of mounted men, an equal distance apart and traveling in the same general direction—like a round-up sweeping over a cattle-range.

"They're out for somebody. I shouldn't be surprised if they have smelled out our friends," said MacRae. "And seeing this bunch is heading right toward us, we might as well take it easy here till they come up."

Returning to the cool shade, we waited till they crossed that miniature desert. I looked once or twice, and hoped we would not have to walk over it; I'd seen the Mohave and the Staked Plains, and I knew it was sizzling hot in that ancient river-bed—it *is* hot, and dry, when the heat-waves play tricks with objects seen from afar. Those three riders moved in a transparent haze, distorted, grotesque figures; now giants, broad, uncouth shapes; now pigmies astride of horses that progressed slowly on long, stiltlike legs, again losing form and waving like tall, slender trees swayed by vagrant winds. After a time they ascended above the level where the superheated atmosphere played its pranks, and came riding up the ridge in their true presentment. When they got within shouting distance we stepped into the sunlight and hailed them.

From the moment that they jerked up their horses at MacRae's call, I had an odd sense of impending trouble. For an instant it seemed as if they were about to break for cover; and when they approached us there was a strained, expectant expression on each tanned face, a wariness in their actions that looked unnatural to me. The nearer they came the more did I feel keyed up for some emergency. I can't explain why; that's something that I don't think will bear logical analysis. Who can explain the sixth sense that warns a night-herder of a stampede a moment before the herd jumps off the bed-ground? But that is how I felt—and immediately it transpired that there was good reason.

They stopped their horses within ten feet of us and dismounted, all three of them, a corporal and two privates, in the same breath that we said "hello." The corporal, rather chalky-looking under his tan, stepped forward and laid a hand on MacRae's shoulder.

"Gordon MacRae and Sarge Flood, in the Queen's name I arrest you for the robbery of Paymaster Ingstram on the MacLeod trail and the murder of two of his escort, and I warn you that anything you may say will be used against you."

He poured it out without pause or inflection, like a lesson well learned, a little ceremony of speech that it was well to hurry over; and the two troopers edged nearer, the right hand of each stealing toward the pistol that rested on his hip. It took nerve to beard us that way, when one comes to think it over. If we had been guilty of that raid, it was dollars to doughnuts that we would resist arrest, and according to the rules and regulations of the Force, they were compelled to take a long chance. A Mounted Policeman can't use his gun except in self-defense. He isn't supposed to smoke up a fugitive unless the fugitive begins to throw lead his way—which method of procedure gives a man who is, in the vernacular, "on the dodge" all the best of a situation like that; for it gives an outlaw a chance to take the initiative, and the first shot often settles an argument of that kind. The dominating idea, as I understood it, was that the majesty of the law should prove a sufficiently powerful weapon; and in the main it did. No thief, murderer, or smuggler ever yet successfully and systematically defied it. Men have gone to the bad up there—robbed, murdered, defrauded, killed a Policeman or two, maybe, but in the end were gathered in by "the riders of the plains" and dealt with according to their just deserts. So it has come to pass throughout the length and breadth of the Northwest that "in the Queen's name" out of the mouth of an unarmed redcoat, with one hand lightly on your shoulder, carries more weight than a smoking gun.

None of this occurred to me, just then. The one thing that loomed big in my mind's eye was the monstrous injustice of the accusation. Coming right on top of what I'd lately experienced at the hands of the men who had really done that dirty job—my head still tingled from the impact of Hicks' pistol—it stirred up all the ugliness I was capable of, and a lot that I had never suspected. No Fort Walsh guardhouse for me! No lying behind barred windows, with my feet chain-hobbled like a straying horse, while the slow-moving Canadian courts debated my guilt or innocence! Not while I had the open prairie underfoot and the summer sky above, and hands to strike a blow or pull a trigger.

Even had I been alone I think that I was crazy enough, for the moment, to have matched myself single-handed against the three of them. In which case I should likely have bidden a premature farewell to all earthly interests—though I might, perhaps, have managed to take with me a Policeman or two for company on the long trail. But a queer look that flashed over MacRae's face, a suggestive drawing back of his arm, intimated that something of the same was in his mind. Heavens, but a man can think a lot in the space of time it takes to count three!

I jumped for the two troopers, with a frenzied notion that I could put them both out of business if MacRae would only attend to the corporal. The distance didn't permit of gun-play; and, hot as I was, I had the sense to know that those men weren't responsible for my troubles; I didn't want to kill them, if I could help it—what I desired above all else was to get away, and burn powder with Hicks, Gregory and Co., if powder-burning was to be on the programme. They did try to pull their guns, but I was too close. I spoiled their good intentions by kicking one with all the force I could muster, and throwing my arms in a fervent embrace about the neck of the other.

A number eight box-toed riding-boot planted suddenly in the pit of one's stomach brings about the same result as a kick from a vigorous Missouri mule, I should imagine; anyway, that Mounted Policeman was eliminated as a fighting unit from the instant my toe made connections with his person. The other fellow and I went to the ground, and our struggle was of short duration, for Mac bought into the ruction with his carbine for a club, and under its soothing touch my wiry antagonist ceased from troubling. I scrambled to my feet and glanced around. The corporal was sprawled on the grass, his face to the sky.

"We've burned our bridges now, sure as fate," Mac broke out. "Here, I'll peel the guns off the bunch, and you lead their horses up to the rock out of sight of these other fellows. If they catch sight of us milling around here they're apt to swing over this way to see what's up."

I led the horses close to the boulder and left them standing there while I hurried back. By that time the fellow I'd kicked had so far recovered as to sit up, and the look he gave us was a scorcher. MacRae, with cocked carbine to emphasize his command, ordered him to drag his comrade to where the horses stood; and I followed after, lugging the insensible corporal to the same shady place.

"I want to know the how of this," Mac demanded of the trooper. "Who issued orders for our arrest on this damn fool charge? And when?"

"Lessard give us our orders," the Policeman growled. "He's been out with a whole bloomin' troop ever since he got word the paymaster 'ad bin stuck up. We got a commissary along, an' nooned about ten miles east o' here. After dinner—about two or three hours ago—he lined us up an' said as 'ow he'd got word that you two fellers 'ad bin identified as bein' the chaps as pulled off that paymaster row, an' that he wanted you. Said he 'ad reason t' believe you was some'ers between Lost River an' the Stone, an' you was t' be captured without fail. An' that's all I know about it," he concluded frankly, "except that you fellers is bloody fools t' make a break like this. It'll go that much 'arder with you—there ain't a bloomin' chance for you t' get away. You might just as well give up peaceable."

"Oh, don't preach," MacRae protested. "I know all that as well as you do. Great Scott! Burky, you've known me ever since I joined; do you imagine for a minute that I was in on that hold-up? Why, you know better. If I'd done anything so damned rotten, I'd have been out of the country long before this."

"Orders is orders," Burky sententiously observed. "Headquarters sez you're t' be took in, an' you'll be took in, no matter what a feller's private opinion happens t' be. I ain't no bloomin' judge an' jury t' set on your case, anyway. You'll get a square trial—same as everybody gets. But you ain't a-helpin' yourself a-cuttin' of didoes like this."

Raw Gold

"I haven't time to go into details," Mac told him, "and I don't suppose you'd believe me if I did. But I've a blamed good reason for not wanting to put in several months cooling my heels under guard while the men that got the stuff get clear out of the country. We're going to take two of these horses, because we'll need them in our business; and we'll leave your guns at that big rock down the ridge. I don't want to hurt you, Burky, but if you start making signals to the rest of the bunch before we get out of sight, you'll go back to Walsh feet first. So be good. You'll see us again before long."

When we were ready to mount, MacRae fired another question at Burky. "Say, have you seen anything of Frank Hicks or Paul Gregory to-day?"

"They was both in camp at noon," the trooper replied.

"Huh! They were, eh?" MacRae swung up, and spoke from the saddle. "Well, if you see them again, tell them we'll sure give them a hard run for the money. And if you've got your month's pay on you, Burky, you'd better keep your hand on it while those two pilgrims are about."

We took the third horse along as a precautionary measure. At a boulder down the ridge we left him, together with their belts, as Mac had promised. The only bit of their property we kept besides the horses was a pair of field-glasses—something that we knew would be priceless to men who were practically outlawed. For the next two hours we slunk like coyotes in coulée-bottoms and deep washouts, until we saw the commissary wagon cross the ridge west of Lost River, saw from a safe distance the brown specks that were riders, casting in wide circles for sight of us or our trail.

Then MacRae leaned over his saddle-horn and made a wry face at them.

"Hunt, confound you," he said, almost cheerfully. "We'll give you some hunting to do before you're through with us."

CHAPTER XIV.

A CLOSE CALL.

We were standing in a brushy pocket on the side of a hill, and as there was no immediate danger of our being seen, MacRae continued, by the aid of the glasses, to follow the movements of our would-be captors.

"D'you know that plunder can't be far away; those fellows haven't had much time to make their *cache*," he reflected, more to himself than to me. "I wonder how they accounted to Lessard for us. Just think of it—somewhere within twenty miles of us there's in the neighborhood of a hundred thousand dollars of stolen money, planted till they can get it safely; and the men that got away with it are helping the law to run us down. That's a new feature of the case; one, I must say, that I didn't look for."

He lowered the glasses, and regarded me soberly.

"They fight fire with fire in a grass country," he observed. "The Mounted Police are a hard formation to buck against—but I've a mind to see this thing to a finish. How do you feel about it, Sarge? Will you go through?"

"All the way and back again," I promised recklessly. I wasn't sure of what he had in mind, but I knew *him*—and seeing that we were in the same boat, I thought it fitting that we should sink or swim together.

"We'll come out on top yet," he confidently asserted. "Meantime we'd better locate some secluded spot and give our nags a chance to fill up on grass and be fresh for to-morrow; we're apt to have a hard day."

"It wouldn't be a bad scheme to fill ourselves at the same time," I suggested. "I'm feeling pretty vacant inside. The first bunch of buffalo that has a fat calf along is going to hear from me."

"If we can get over this ridge without being seen, there's a canyon with some cottonwoods and a spring in it. That will be as good a place to hole up for the night as we can find," Mac decided. "And there will likely be some buffalo near there."

So we ascended cautiously to the top of the divide, keeping in the coulées as much as possible, for we knew that other field-glasses would be focused on the hills. Once over the crest, we halted and watched for riders coming our way. But none appeared. Once I thought I glimpsed a moving speck on the farther bank of Lost River. MacRae brought the glasses to bear, and said it was two Policemen jogging toward camp. Then we were sure that our flight had not been observed, and we dropped into a depression that gradually deepened to a narrow-bottomed canyon. Two miles down this we came to the spring of which MacRae had spoken, a tiny stream issuing from a crevice at the foot of the bank. What was equally important, a thick clump of cottonwood and willow furnished tolerably secure concealment.

The fates smiled on us in the matter of food very shortly. I'm not enamored of a straight meat diet as a rule, but that evening I was in no mood to carp at anything half-way eatable. While we were on our stomachs gratefully stowing away a draught of the cool water, I heard a buffalo bull lift his voice in challenge to another far down the canyon. We tied our horses out of sight in the timber and stole in the direction of the sound. A glorious bull-fight was taking place when we got within shooting-distance, the cows and calves forming a noisy circle about the combatants, each shaggy brown brute bawling with all the strength of bovine lungs; in that pandemonium of bellowing and trampling I doubt if the report of Mac's carbine could have been heard two hundred yards away. The shot served to break up the fight and scatter the herd, however, and we returned to the cottonwoods with the hind-quarter of a fat calf.

Hungry as we were, we could hardly bolt raw meat, so, taking it for granted that no one was likely to ride up on us, we built a fire in the grove, being careful to feed it with dry twigs that would make little smoke. Over this we toasted bits of meat on the end of a splinter, and presently our hunger was appeased. Then we blotted out the fire, and, stretching ourselves on the ground, had recourse to the solace of tobacco.

The longer we laid there the more curious did I become as to what line of action MacRae purposed to follow. He lay on his back, silent, staring straight up at the bit of sky that showed through the branches above, and I'd just reached the point of asking, when he sat up and forestalled my questions.

"This is going to be risky business, Sarge," he began. "But so far as I can see, there is only one way that we can hope to get the thing straightened out. If we can get hold of Hicks or Bevans, any one of the four, in fact, I think we can *make* him tell us all we need to know. It's the only chance for you and Lyn to get your money back, and for me to square myself."

"I shouldn't think," I put in resentfully, "that you'd want to square yourself, after the dirty way you've been treated. I'd as soon take to herding sheep, or washing dirty clothes like a Chinaman, as be a member of the Mounted Police if what I've seen in the last ten days is a fair sample of what a man can expect."

"Fiddlesticks!" Mac impatiently exclaimed. "You don't know what you're talking about. I tell you a man in the Police, if he has any head at all, can control his own destiny. You'll be a heap more sane when you get that old, wild-west notion, that every man should be a law unto himself, out of your head. I'll venture to say that the Northwest will be a safer and more law-abiding place five years from now than south of the line will be in twenty—and the men in red coats will make it so. Why, I wouldn't miss helping tame this country for half a dozen such scrapes as I'm in now. This is merely the result of a rotten spot in the personnel, a rotten spot that will soon be cut out if things come about logically; it isn't the fault of the system. There never was any great movement in developing a new country that didn't have a quota of damned rascals to eliminate from within itself. If you didn't have such a perverted idea of independence, you'd see that I'm in no danger of losing either my identity or my self-respect simply because I've become a unit in a body of six hundred fighting-men. I don't intend to remain in the insignificant-unit class."

"Your intentions," I interrupted, "will cut a mighty small figure if your friend Lessard gets hold of you in the next day or two."

"That's the melancholy truth," he returned seriously. "I imagine we'd get a pretty rough deal; in fact, I wouldn't be surprised if that troop has received orders, by now, to shoot first and arrest afterward. Still, I'm willing to gamble that if we rode into Fort Walsh and gave ourselves up, it would only be a matter of a few weeks in the guardhouse for us before the thing was cleared up."

"Maybe," I responded skeptically. "If that's your belief, why don't you act accordingly?"

"Because, confound it, that's just where they want to get us," he declared. "Once we were safely penned, they'll drift, and neither you nor Lyn Rowan nor the government would ever lay eyes on that bundle of money again. I have a theory—but what's vastly more important, I think those fellows can hardly get out of the country with their plunder without crossing trails with us. It was smooth business to set the dogs on us. I don't quite *sabe*—well, I do, too. You can probably realize just how headquarters would take the sort of yarn we'd spin if we dashed in and told them the truth. But I think we're smart enough to upset these fellows' calculations. Lord! wouldn't it be a stroke of business if we could trap that collection of buccaneers? Frankly, that would be the biggest thing that ever came my way."

"It would be equally a stroke of business if they happen to trap us," I reminded.

"They won't," he asserted confidently. "We can't afford to let them. We've inflicted a compound fracture on established law, and until we can make the outcome justify our actions, we're compelled, in self-defense, to avoid being caught. It may be a dubious undertaking, but as I see it the only thing for us is to hang on the flank of these man-hunters till we can lay hold of one of that red-handed quartette. According to Burky, two of them, at least, are in that troop. Probably the others are. And knowing that bunch as well as I do, I don't think they'll lift the plunder and quit the country till they can go together. Even if we can't get hold of one of them, we can keep track of their movements, and if they *do* lift their *cache* and pull out, why, that would be as good as we want. I wouldn't ask anything better than to get a fair chance at that bunch with the stolen money on them."

I'll admit that, soberly considered, MacRae's plan did look exceeding risky. No one could appreciate better than ourselves the unpleasant possibilities that stared us in the face. But things had narrowed to a point where only two courses were open to us—one, to throw up our hands and quit the jurisdiction of the Mounted Police, which involved desertion on MacRae's part, and on mine a chicken-hearted abandonment of La Pere's trust in me (for, rightly or wrongly, I was given over to the feeling that on me alone rested the responsibility for the loss or recovery of La Pere's money); the other, to take any measure, no matter how desperate, that would unravel the tangle. All things considered, the latter was the logical choice. And the plan Mac had put forth seemed as feasible as any.

"We'll have to proceed on the faro-bank formula that all bets go as they lay," I said lightly. "There's no use anticipating things disagreeable or otherwise; we'll simply have to take them as they come."

By this time dusk was upon us. We picketed the horses in the open bottom where grass was more plentiful than in the brush, and settled ourselves to sleep. Fortunately, the aftermath of that blistering day was a fairly warm night. By spreading over us the heavy woolen blankets the Mounted Police use under their saddles, we slept in comfort. Long before dawn, however, we arose, built a fire, and breakfasted on buffalo veal, at the same time broiling a good supply and stowing it in our pockets to serve the rest of the day. Then, with darkness still obscuring our movements, we saddled and rode over the ridge and down into Lost River, crossing that ancient waterway before the first glimmer of light in the east.

Day found us dismounted in the head of a coulée where we could spy on the Police camp from a distance of three miles, more or less. About sunrise the troop left camp in a body, later spreading fanwise over the prairies. Once a party trotted by within a half-mile of us, but no one of the four men we wanted to see was in the squad.

Until after the noon hour we laid *perdu* in the hollow, no wiser for our watching. Then I saw a number of riders debouch from the camp, and at once trained the glasses on them. At first I couldn't distinguish any particular face among so many shifting forms, but presently they split in two bodies, and these again subdivided; and in the bunch coming toward us I recognized three men, Lessard, unmistakable in his black uniform, Hicks, and Bevans. I turned the glasses over to MacRae then.

"I thought probably some more of our friends would show up," he said, after a quick survey. "With those two in sight the chances are that all four are with the troop. The other fellows in that squad are just plain buck Policemen. Confound them, I wish——Aha, by Jupiter! the big chief is turning off those two."

As Mac spoke I saw the two men I had spotted as Hicks and Bevans swing away from the rest and angle toward Lost River. From our vantage point we watched them come abreast and pass us at a distance well within a mile. The others turned south, directly away from us.

"Now," Mac coolly declared, "here's where we get the chance we want, if we're lucky. We'll keep parallel with these gentlemen, and if they get out of touch with the rest we'll make a try at nailing them. Be careful, though, how you show yourself; there's at least fifty of these peacemakers within four or five miles, and a shot or a yell will bring them on a high run."

Hicks and Bevans, whatever their destination, were in no haste. They rode at a walk most of the time, and we were forced to keep the same pace. It was slow work poking along those coulée-bottoms, now and then making a risky sneak to ground, whence we could get a clear view of the game we were stalking so assiduously.

Progressing in this manner we finally reached the breaks that ran down to Lost River, not a great distance from where MacRae and I had kicked over the traces of legally constituted authority the previous day. Here we had to dodge over a stretch of ground barren of concealment, and to do so waited till such time as Hicks and Bevans were themselves in the depths of a coulée.

When next we caught sight of our men—well, to be exact, we saw only one, and that was Bevans. He had stopped his horse on top of a knoll not more than four hundred yards to the north of us, and was standing up in his stirrups staring over the ears of his horse at a point down the slope. Hicks had disappeared. Nor did we see aught of him during the next few minutes that we spent glaring at Bevans and the surrounding territory.

"I wonder if that square-jawed devil has got a glimpse of us and is trying a lone-handed stalk himself?" I hazarded.

MacRae shook his head. "Not likely," he said. "If it was Paul Gregory, now, that's the very thing he'd do. I don't quite *sabe* this performance."

We watched for sign of Hicks, but without result. Then Bevans got under way and moved along at the same poky gait as before. When he had gone some distance we took to the hollow. Twenty minutes jogging brought us into a stretch of rough country, a series of knobs and ridges cut by innumerable coulées. Here it became necessary to locate Mr. Bevans again. Once more he was revealed on top of an elevation, studying the surrounding landscape, and he was still alone.

"Where the mischief can Hicks have got to?" Mac growled. "We really ought to smell him out before we do anything."

"Look, now," I said. "Don't you suppose Bevans is waiting for him?"

Bevans had dismounted and stretched himself on the ground in the shade of his horse. But he was not napping; on the contrary, he was very much on the alert, for his head turned slowly from side to side, quiescent as he seemed; there would be little movement pass unobserved within range of that pair of eyes.

"Maybe he is," MacRae replied. "Anyhow, I think we'd better wait a while ourselves."

For nearly an hour Bevans kept his position. Hicks, if he were in the vicinity, kept closely under cover. Bevans had all the best of the situation, so far as being able to keep a lookout was a factor; the opposite bank of the coulée we were in towered high above us, and shut off our view in that direction. And we didn't dare risk showing ourselves on high ground. Finally, after what seemed an interminable period of waiting, Mac's patience frazzled out and he declared for action.

"We're doing no good here," he said. "Hicks or no Hicks, I'm going to have a try at making connections with his nibs on that hill. I think the coulée right under his perch is an arm of the one we're in; runs in somewhere below. Maybe we can get to him that way. It's worth trying."

As MacRae had surmised, our canyon forked below. We turned the point after making sure that Bevans couldn't see us unless he moved. But the uncertain beggar had moved, and moved to some purpose we quickly learned; for when we next laid eyes on him he was out on the extreme point of the little bench, opposite the mouth of the coulée we had ascended, whirling his horse about in cramped circles.

And in answer to his signaling a full score of red-jacketed riders were galloping down the ridges, a human comb that bade fair to rake us from our concealment in a scant number of minutes.

"Looks bad for you and me, old boy," MacRae grinned. "I see now what brother Hicks has been up to. But they haven't got us yet. Whatever happens, Sarge, don't get excited and go to shooting. We can't win out that way, against this combination. If we can't dodge and outrun them we'll have to take our medicine. Down the coulée is our only chance. There's only Bevans to stop us; and it won't really matter if we do put his light out—be one thief less at the finish."

Bevans, however, made no demonstration. We just got a mere glimpse of him, and I imagine he was nowise anxious to try heading us off, which he could not do without coming into the open. Whipping around the crooked bends at top speed, he had little chance to pot us, and I think he had an idea that we would cheerfully pot him if he got in the way.

We mystified them somewhat, and gained considerable ground, by that sudden dash, but it wasn't long before they were in full cry like a pack of hounds, and the carbines began to pop in a futile sort of way. Mac had not been far astray when he hazarded the guess that the troop would have orders to shoot on sight, for they began to peck at us the moment we came in view. We had just enough of a start, though, and our mounts were just good enough and fresh enough to gradually draw away from them. And as we were then out of the network of protecting coulées and pattering over the comparative level of Lost River bottoms, I was very glad that we were beyond carbine-range and that it was near sundown.

"Barring accidents, they can't get up on us now," Mac declared. "So I think it'll be wise to keep south along the open bottoms. If they see us splitting the breeze down Lost River, they won't look for us to bob up from the opposite quarter to-morrow. When it gets dark and we're far enough ahead, we can swing into the hills. That'll fool them plenty for to-night. They'll probably try tracking us to-morrow, but I reckon they'll find that a tough job."

They kept persistently after us, and we were more or less on the anxious seat, till it did get dark. Then we turned sharp to the left and gained high ground once more, congratulating ourselves on so easily getting out of a ticklish place. If we hadn't moved up on Bevans they might have surrounded us before we got wind of them. But we'd beaten them fairly, and so we looked back through the dark and laughed; though I'm sure we had no particular cause for merriment.

CHAPTER XV.

PIEGAN TAKES A HAND.

I don't believe a detailed account of how we spent that night would be classed as wildly interesting; if memory serves me right, it was a bleak, hungry, comfortless passage of time, and I am willing to let it go at that. We managed to secure a buffalo steak for breakfast. No man needed to starve in that country during those days of plentiful game; but we were handicapped by the necessity of doing our hunting in a very surreptitious manner. However, we didn't starve; the worst we experienced was an occasional period of acute hunger, when we didn't dare fire a shot for fear of revealing our whereabouts.

Nor can I see, now, where we accomplished anything beyond killing time the following day. To be sure, we scouted faithfully, and once or twice came perilously near being caught by squads of Mounted Police appearing from unexpected quarters. Our scouting was so much wasted energy. We got nowhere near the Police camp; we failed to get a glimpse of any of our men; and so, for all we knew to the contrary, they might have loaded the plunder and decamped for other regions. When night again spread its concealing folds about us, we had only one tangible fact as a reward for our exertions—Lessard had returned to Fort Walsh—presumably. Early that morning, escorted by four troopers, he had crossed Lost River and disappeared in the direction of the post. Of his identity the field-glasses assured us. But that was the sum total of our acquired knowledge, and it brought us no nearer the breaking up of the Goodell-Gregory combination or the recovery of the loot.

So for a third night we were compelled to seek sanctuary in the silent canyons. And the third day brought us no better luck. At evening we were constrained to admit that we were simply butting our heads against a wall—with an ever-present possibility of the wall toppling over and crushing us flat.

Altogether, we spent five consecutive days hovering around that collection of law-enforcers, in imminent risk of capture. Each night in the open was more cheerless than the preceding one, and each day brought the same sense of futile effort at its close. Twice during that time the Police camp moved, and we had to be wary, for they scoured the surrounding territory with painstaking thoroughness. But we felt that there was yet a chance for us to turn the tables, for Goodell was still with the troop, and also Gregory; we saw them both the morning of the fifth day.

"It beats me why they're pecking around over the same ground so much," Mac observed. "I suppose they're looking for us, but I'm pretty sure they haven't had a glimpse of us for three days, and so I don't see why they should think we're still hanging around. Logically, if we'd got that bunch of money, we'd be getting out of the country. Lord, I do wish those four would show their hand — make a move of some kind."

"So do I," I seconded. "We're not doing much good that I can see. And I think I could play the game with a heap more enthusiasm if I had some coffee and white bread under my belt once or twice a day. We'll go hungry, and likewise get a devilish good soaking to-night, or I'm badly mistaken."

We had checked our horses on the summit of the divide that ran down to Lost River on one side and on the other sloped away to the southeast. The wind that was merely a breath at sundown had gathered strength to itself and now swept across the hill-tops with a resonant roar, piling layer on layer of murky low-flying clouds into a dense mass overhead. Night, black as the bottomless pit, walled us in. A fifty-mile breeze lashed us spitefully, tugging at our shirt-sleeves and drowning our voices, while we halted on that pinnacle. By the dank breath of the wind, the ominous overcasting of the sky, all the little signs that a prairie-wise man learns to read, we knew that a storm was close at hand. Shelter there was none, nor food, and we stood in need of both.

"You're right," MacRae admitted. "But how are we going to help it? We'll just have to grin and tough it out."

"I'll tell you how we'll help it," I proposed recklessly, shouting to make myself heard above the noisy wind. "We can go down and tackle that bull-train we saw pulling along the foot of the ridge. They'll know we're on the dodge, but that won't make any difference to them. I know nearly every bull-whacker that freights out of Benton, and they're a pretty white bunch. If it's Baker's outfit, especially, we'll be welcome as flowers in May. You said they'd likely camp at that spring—Ten Mile, isn't it? What d'ye think? Shall we go down and take a chance? I sure don't like the look of things up here. It's going to be a rip-snorter of a night, once it cuts loose."

"I'm ready to go against nearly anything, right now," MacRae frankly owned. "If you think it's worth trying, why, it's a go with me."

"Let's drift, then," I declared; and straightway we turned our horses broadside to the wind and tore away for Ten Mile Spring and the creature comforts I knew were to be had at the white-sheeted wagons we saw crawling slowly along the Stony Crossing trail late that afternoon.

As Mac had calculated, the freight-train was camped at the Spring; and it was a mighty good thing for us that MacRae knew that country so well or we would never have found them, short of riding our horses to a standstill. Long before we got there the deep-throated thunder was growling over us, and the clouds spat occasional flurries of rain.

We made the freight camp, however, just as the storm cut loose in deadly earnest. Luckily for me, it was Baker's outfit. I took a long chance, and stalked boldly in. And here I was treated to a surprise, one that afforded both MacRae and me considerable food for thought; Horner, the wagon-boss, a man I knew well, frankly declared that no one at Fort Walsh had heard that we were accused of robbery and murder. For that matter, he said, he didn't care a tinker's dam if we were; he had grub and bedding and we were welcome to both.

So with this assurance of good-will we picketed our horses close by the circle of wagons—where we could get to them quickly should any of Lessard's troop happen into the camp—and prepared to devour the supper Horner's good-natured cook bestirred himself to make ready. As we filled our plates and squatted under the canvas that sheltered the cook's Dutch-oven layout, a man under the hind end of the chuck-wagon propped himself on elbow and shouted greeting to us. In the semi-dark I couldn't see his face, but I recognized the voice. It was our friend of the whisky-keg episode, Piegan Smith.

"Hello, thar, fellers!" he bellowed (Piegan always spoke to a man as if he were a hundred yards away). "Say, Flood, yuh ain't been t' Benton an' back already, have yuh?"

"Faith, no," I owned, between mouthfuls, "and it's hard telling when I will get there. How come you to be pacing along this trail, Piegan? Gone to freighting in your old age?"

"Not what yuh could notice, I ain't," he snorted. "Catch *me* whackin' bulls for a livin'! Naw, I sold my outfit to a goggle-eyed pilgrim that has an idea buffalo hides is prime all summer. So I'm headed for Benton to see if I kain't stir up a little excitement now an' then, to pass away the time till the fall buffalo-run begins."

"If you're looking for excitement, Piegan," MacRae put in dryly, "you'd better come along with us. We'll introduce you to more different brands of it in the next few days than Benton could furnish in six months."

"Maybe," Piegan laughed. "But not the brand I'm a-thirstin' for."

Mac was on the point of replying when there came a most unexpected interruption. I looked up at sound of a startled exclamation, and beheld the round African physog of Lyn Rowan's colored mammy. But she had no eyes for me; she stood like a black statue just within the firelight, a tin bucket in one hand, staring over my head at MacRae.

"Lawd a-me!" she gulped out. "Ef Ah ain't sho'ly laid mah ol' eyes on Marse Go'don. Is dat sho' 'nuf yo', wid yo' red coat an' all?"

"It sure is, Mammy," Mac answered. "How does it happen you're traveling this way? I thought you were at Fort Walsh. Is Miss Lyn along?"

"She suttinly am," Mammy Thomas emphatically asserted. "Yo' doan catch dis chile a-mosyin' obeh dese yeah plains by huh lonesome. Since dey done brought Miss Lyn's paw in an' planted him, she say dey ain't no use foh huh to stay in dis yeah redcoat country no longer; so we all packed up an' sta'ted back foh de lan' ob de free."

MacRae, I am sure, was no more than half through his meal. But he swallowed the coffee in his cup, and tossed his eating-implements into the cook's wash-pan.

"I'll go with you, Mammy," he told her. "I want to see Miss Lyn myself."

"Jes' a minute, Marse Go'don," she said. "Ah's got to git some wa'm watah f'om dis yeah Mr. Cook."

The cook signaled her to help herself from the kettle that bubbled over the fire, and she filled her bucket and disappeared, chattering volubly, MacRae at her heels.

I finished my supper more deliberately. There was no occasion for me to gobble my food and rush off to talk with Lyn Rowan. MacRae, I suspected, would be inclined to monopolize her for the rest of the evening. So I ate leisurely, and when done crawled under the wagon beside Piegan Smith and gave myself up to cigarettes and meditation, while over his pipe Piegan expressed a most unflattering opinion of the weather.

It was a dirty night, beyond question; one that gave color to Piegan's prophesy that Milk River would be out of its banks if the storm held till morning, and that Baker's freight-train would be stalled by mud and high water for three or four days. I was duly thankful for the shelter we had found. A tarpaulin stretched from wheel to wheel of the wagon shut out the driving rain that fled in sheets before the whooping wind. The lightning-play was hidden behind the drifting cloud-bank, for no glint of it penetrated the gloom; but the cavernous thunder-bellow roared intermittently, and a fury of rain drove slantwise against sodden earth and creaking wagon-tops.

If the next two hours were as slow in passing, to MacRae and Lyn, as they seemed to me, the two of them had time to dissect and discuss the hopes and fears and errors of their whole existence, and formulate a new philosophy of life. Piegan broke a long silence to remark sagely that if Mac was putting in all this time talking to that "yaller-headed fairy," he was a plumb good stayer.

"They're old friends," I told him. "Mac knew her long ago; and all her people."

"Well, he's in darned agreeable company," Piegan observed. "She's a mighty fine little woman, far's I've seen. I dunno's I'd know when t' jar loose m'self, if I knowed her an' she didn't object t' me hangin' around. But seein' we ain't in on the reception, we might as well get under the covers, eh? I reckon most everybody in camp's turned in."

Piegan had a bulky roll of bedding under the wagon. Spread to its full width, it was ample for three ordinary men. We had just got out of our outside garments and were snuggling down between the blankets when Mac came slopping through the puddles that were now gathering in every depression. He crawled under the wagon, shed some of his clothing, and got into bed with us. But he didn't lie down until he had rolled a cigarette, and then instead of going to sleep he began talking to Piegan, asking what seemed to me a lot of rather trifling questions. I was nearly worn out, and their conversation was nowise interesting to me, so listening to the monotonous drone of their voices and the steady beat of falling rain, I went to sleep.

Before a great while I wakened; to speak truthfully, the ungentle voice of Piegan Smith brought me out of dreamland with a guilty start. MacRae was still sitting up in bed, and from that part of his speech which filtered into my ears I gathered that he was recounting to Piegan the tale of our adventures during the past week. I thought that odd, for Mac was a close-mouthed beggar as a general thing; but there was no valid reason why he should not proclaim the story from the hill-tops if he chose, so I rolled over and pulled the blankets above my head—to protect my ear-drums if Piegan's astonishment should again find verbal expression.

The cook's battle-cry of "Grub *pi-i-ile*" wakened me next. A thin line of yellowish-red in the east betokened the birth of another day, a day born in elemental turmoil, for the fierce wind was no whit abated, nor the sullen, driving rain.

"I've enlisted a recruit," MacRae told me in an undertone, as we ate breakfast. "It struck me that if we had somebody along that we could trust to ride into that Police camp with his mouth shut and his ears and eyes open, we might find out something that would show us how the land lay; even if he accomplished nothing else, he could learn if those fellows are still with the troop."

"That was why you were making that talk to Piegan last night, was it?" I said. "Well, from what little I've seen and heard of him, he'd be a whole team if he's willing to throw in with us and take a chance." Which was perfectly true. Old Piegan had the reputation, on both sides of the line, of loving to jump into a one-sided fight for the pure joy of evening up the odds. He was a boisterous, rough-spoken mortal, but his heart was big, and set in the right place. And, though I didn't know it then, he had a grouch against Hicks, who had once upon a time run him into Fort Walsh in irons on an unjustified suspicion of whisky-running. That was really what started Piegan in the smuggling business—a desire to play even, after getting what he called a "damn rough deal."

"He's willing enough," Mac assured me. "Aside from the fact that most any white man would go out of his way to help a girl like Lyn Rowan, there's the certainty that the Canadian government will be pretty generous to anybody who helps round up that crooked bunch and restore the stolen money. Piegan snorted when I told him we were on the dodge—that they were trying to nail us for holding up the paymaster. That's the rottenest part of the whole thing. I think— but then we've got to do more than think to get ourselves out of this jackpot."

He stopped abruptly, and went on with his breakfast. By the time we were done eating, the gray light of a bedraggled morning revealed tiny lakes in every hollow, and each coulée and washout was a miniature torrent of muddy water—with a promise of more to come in the murky cloud-drift that overcast the sky. Horner sent out two men to relieve the night-herders, remarked philosophically "More rain, more rest," and retired to the shelter of the cook's canvas. His drivers sought cover in and under the wagons, where they had spent the night. But though mud and swollen streams might hold back the cumbrous freight outfit, it did not follow that heavy going would delay the flitting of the thieves, if they planned such a move; nor would it prevent the Mounted Police from descending on the Baker outfit if they thought we had taken refuge there. So we held council of war with Piegan, after which we saddled up and made ready to tackle the soaked prairies.

While we were packing grub and bedding on Piegan's extra horse, Lyn joined us, wrapped from head to heel in a yellow slicker. And by the way Mac greeted her I knew that they had bridged that gap of five years to their mutual satisfaction; that she was loath to see him set out on a hazardous mission she presently made plain.

"Let it go, Gordon," she begged. "There's been too much blood shed over that wretched gold already. Let them have it. I know something dreadful will happen if you follow it up."

"THERE'S BEEN TOO MUCH BLOOD SHED OVER THAT
WRETCHED GOLD ALREADY. LET THEM HAVE IT."

MacRae smiled and shook his head stubbornly. "I'm too deep in, little woman, to quit now," he told her patiently. "If it was only a matter of your money, we could get along without it. But Sarge stands to lose a lot, if we give up at this stage of the game. And besides, I'd always be more or less on the dodge if this thing isn't cleared up. I've got to see it through. You wouldn't have me sneak out of this country like a whipped pup, would you? There's too big an account to settle with those fellows, Lyn; it's up to us, if we're men. I can't draw back now, till it's settled for good and all, one way or the other."

"Oh, I know how you feel about it," she sighed. "But even if it comes out all right, you're still tied here. You know they won't let you go."

"Don't you worry about that," he comforted. "I'll cross that bridge fast enough when I come to it. You go on to Benton, like a good girl. I feel it in my bones that we're going to have better luck from now on. And if we do, you'll see us ride down the Benton hill one of these fine mornings. Anyway, I'll send you word by Piegan before long."

Piegan was already mounted, watching us whimsically from under the dripping brim of his hat. I shook hands with Lyn, and swung into my saddle. And when Mac had kissed her, we crowded through a gap in the circle of wagons, waved a last good-by, and rode away in the steadily falling rain.

CHAPTER XVI.

IN THE CAMP OF THE ENEMY.

From then until near noon we worked our passage if ever men did. On the high benches it was not so bad for the springy, porous turf soaked up the excessive moisture and held its firmness tolerably well. But every bank of any steepness meant a helter-skelter slide to its foot, with either a bog-hole or swimming water when we got there, and getting up the opposite hill was like climbing a greased pole—except that there was no purse at the top to reward our perseverance. Between the succeeding tablelands lay gumbo flats where the saturated clay hung to the feet of our horses like so much glue, or opened under hoof-pressure and swallowed them to the knees. So that our going was slow and wearisome.

About mid-day the storm gradually changed from unceasing downpour to squally outbursts, followed by banks of impenetrable fog that would shut down on us solidly for a few minutes, then vanish like the good intentions of yesterday; the wind switched a few points and settled to a steady gale which lashed the spent clouds into hurrying ships of the air, scudding full-sail before the droning breeze. Before long little patches of blue began to peep warily through narrow spaces above. The wind-blown rain-makers lost their leaden hue and became a soft pearl-gray, all fleecy white around the edges. Then bars of warm sunshine poured through the widening rifts and the whole rain-washed land lay around us like a great checker-board whereon black cloud-shadows chased each other madly over prairies yellow with the hot August sun and gray-green in the hollows where the grass took on a new lease of life.

That night we camped west of Lost River, lying prudently in a brush-grown coulée, for we were within sight of the Police camp—by grace of the field-glasses. At sundown the ground had dried to such a degree that a horse could lift foot without raising with it an abnormal portion of the Northwest. The wind veered still farther to the south, blowing strong and warm, sucking greedily the surplus moisture from the saturated earth. So we resolved ourselves into a committee of ways and means and decided that since the footing promised to be normal in the morning the troop would likely scatter out, might even move camp, and therefore it behooved us to get in touch with them at once; accordingly Piegan rode away to spend the night in the Police tents, with a tale of horses strayed from Baker's outfit to account for his wandering. From our nook in the ridge he could easily make it by riding a little after dark.

"Goodell and Gregory and Hicks you know," said MacRae. "Bevans is a second edition of Hicks, only not so tall by two or three inches—a square-shouldered, good-looking brute, with light hair and steel-gray eyes and a short brown mustache. He has an ugly scar—a knife-cut—across the back of one hand; you can't mistake him if you get sight of him. Stick around the camp in the morning if you can manage it, till they start, and notice which way all those fellows go. The sooner we get our hands on one or more of them the better we'll be able to get at the bottom of this; I reckon we could find a way to make him talk. Of course, if anything out of the ordinary comes up you'll have to use your own judgment; you know just as much as we do, now. And we'll wait here for you unless they jump us up. In that case we'll try and round up somewhere between here and Ten Mile."

"Right yuh are, old-timer," Piegan responded. "I'll do the best I can. Yuh want t' keep your eye glued t' that peep-glass in the mornin', and not overlook no motions. Yuh kain't tell what might come up. So-long!" And away he went.

When he was gone from sight we built a tiny fire in the scrub—for it was twilight, at which time keen eyes are needed to detect either smoke or fire, except at close range—and cooked our supper. That done, we smothered what few embers remained and laid us down to sleep. That wasn't much of a success, however. We had got into action again, with more of a chance to bring about certain desired results, and inevitably we laid awake reckoning up the chances for and against a happy conclusion to our little expedition.

"It's a wonder," I said, as the thought occurred to me, "that Lyn quit Walsh so soon. Why didn't she stay a while longer and see if these famous preservers of the peace wouldn't manage to gather in the men who killed her father? Why, hang it! she didn't even wait to see if you found that stuff at the Stone—and Lessard must have told her that somebody had gone to look for it."

Mac snapped out an oath in the dark. "Lessard simply lost his head," he growled. "Damn him! He told her that he had sent us to look for it, and that we had taken advantage of the opportunity to rob the paymaster. Oh, he painted us good and black, I tell you. Then he had the nerve to ask her to marry him. And he was so infernally insistent about it, that she was forced to pull up and get away from the post in self-defense. That's why she left so suddenly."

Well, I couldn't find it in my heart to blame Lessard for that last, so long as he acted the gentleman about it. In fact, it was to be expected of almost any man who happened to be thrown in contact with Lyn Rowan for any length of time. I can't honestly lay claim to being absolutely immune myself; only my attack had come years earlier, and had not been virulent enough to make me indulge in any false hopes. It's no crime for an unattached man to care for a woman; but naturally, MacRae would be prejudiced against any one who laid siege to a castle he had marked for his own. I had disliked that big, autocratic major, too, from our first meeting, but it was pure instinctive antipathy on my part, sharpened, perhaps, by his outrageous treatment of MacRae.

We dropped the subject forthwith. Lessard's relation to the problem was a subject we had so far shied around. It was beside the point to indulge in footless theory. We knew beyond a doubt who were the active agents in every blow that had been struck, and the first move in the tangle we sought to unravel was to lay hands on them, violently if necessary, and through them recover the stolen money. Only by having that in our possession—so MacRae argued—could we hope to gain credible hearing, and when that was accomplished whatever part Lessard had played would develop of itself.

By and by, my brain wearied with fruitless speculation, I began to doze, and from then till daylight I slept in five-minute snatches.

Dawn brought an access of caution, and we forbore building a fire. Our horses, which we had picketed in the open overnight, we saddled and tied out of sight in the brush. Then we ate a cold breakfast and betook ourselves to the nearest hill-top, where, screened by a huddle of rocks, we could watch for the coming of Piegan Smith; and, incidentally, keep an eye on the redcoat camp, though the distance was too great to observe their movements with any degree of certainty. The most important thing was to avoid letting a bunch of them ride up on us unheralded.

"They're not setting the earth afire looking for anybody," Mac declared, when the sun was well started on its ante-meridian journey and there was still no sign of riders leaving the cluster of tents. "Ah, there they go."

A squad of mounted men in close formation, so that their scarlet jackets stood out against the dun prairie like a flame in the dark, rode away from the camp, halted on the first hill an instant, then scattered north, south, and west. After that there was no visible stir around the white-sheeted commissary.

"They're not apt to disturb us if they keep going the opposite direction," Mac reflected, his eyes conning them through the glasses. "And neither do they appear to be going to move camp. Therefore, we'll be likely to see Piegan before long."

But it was some time ere we laid eyes on that gentleman. We didn't see him leaving the camp—which occasioned us no uneasiness, because a lone rider could very well get away from there unseen by us, especially if he was circumspect in his choice of routes, as Piegan would probably be. Only when two hours had dragged by, and then two more, did we begin to get anxious. I was lying on my back, staring up at the sky, all sorts of possible misfortune looming large on my mental horizon, when MacRae, sweeping the hills with the glasses, grunted satisfaction, and I turned my head in time to see Piegan appear momentarily on high ground a mile to the south of us.

"What's he doing off there?" I wondered. "Do you suppose somebody's following him, that he thinks it necessary to ride clear around us?"

"Hardly; but you can gamble that he isn't riding for his health," Mac responded. "Anyway, you'll soon know; he's turning."

Piegan swung into the coulée at a fast lope, and we stole carefully down to meet him. In the brush that concealed our horses Piegan dismounted, and, seating himself tailor-fashion on the ground, began to fill his pipe.

"First thing," said he, "we're a little behind the times. Your birds has took wing and flew the coop."

"Took wing—how? And when?" we demanded.

"You'll *sabe* better, I reckon, if I tell yuh just how I made out," Piegan answered, after a pause to light his pipe. "When I got there last night they was most all asleep. But this mornin' I got a chance to size up the whole bunch, and nary one uh them jaspers I wanted t' see was in sight. So whilst we was eatin' breakfast I begins t' quiz, an', one way an' another, lets on I wanted t' see that Injun scout. One feller up an' tells me he guess I'll find the breed at Fort Walsh, most likely. After a while I hears more talk, an' by askin' a few innocent questions I gets next t' some more. Puttin' this an' that together, this here's the way she stacks up: Lessard, as you fellers took notice, went in t' Walsh, takin' several men with him, Gregory bein' among the lot. He leaves orders that these fellers behind are t' comb the country till he calls 'em off. Yesterday mornin', in the thick uh the storm, a buck trooper arrives from Walsh, bearin' instructions for Goodell, Hicks an' another feller, which I reckon is Bevans. So when she clears up a little along towards noon, these three takes a packadero layout an' starts, presumable for Medicine Lodge. An' that's all I found out from the Policemen."

"Scattered them around the country, eh?" Mac commented. "Damn it, we're just as far behind as ever."

"Hold your hosses a minute," Piegan grinned knowingly. "I said that was all I found out from the red jackets—but I did a little prognosticatin' on my own hook. I figured that if them fellers hit the trail yesterday afternoon as soon as the storm let up, they'd make one hell of a good plain track in this sloppy goin' an' I was curious t' see if they lit straight for the Lodge. So when the bunch got out quite a ways, I quits the camp an' swings round in a wide circle—an' sure enough they'd left their mark. Three riders an' two pack-hosses. Easy trackin'? Well, I should say! They'd cut a trail in them doby flats like a bunch uh gallopin' buffalo. Say, where *is* Medicine Lodge?"

"Oh, break away, Piegan," Mac impatiently exclaimed. "What are you trying to get at? You know where the Lodge is as well as I do."

"Well, I always thought I knowed where 'twas," Piegan retorted spiritedly, a wicked twinkle in his shrewd old eyes. "But it must 'a' changed location lately, for them fellers rode north a ways, an' then kept swingin' round till they was headin' due southeast. I follered their trail t' where yuh seen me turn this way, if yuh was watchin'. Poor devils"—Piegan grinned covertly while voicing this mock sympathy—"they must 'a' got lost, I reckon. It really ain't safe for such pilgrims t' be cavortin' over the prairies with all that boodle in their jeans. I reckon we'll just naturally have t' pike along after 'em an' take care of it ourselves. They ain't got such a rip-roarin' start of us—an' I'm the boy can foller that track from hell t' breakfast an' back again. So let's eat a bite, an' then straddle our *caballos* for some tall ridin'."

CHAPTER XVII.

A MASTER-STROKE OF VILLAINY.

Piegan shortly proved that he made no vain boast when he asserted his ability to follow their track. A lifetime on the plains, and a natural fitness for the life, had made him own brother to the Indian in the matter of nosing out dim trails. The crushing of a tuft of grass, a broken twig, all the half-hidden signs that the feet of horses and men leave behind, held a message for him; nothing, however slight, escaped his eagle eye. And he did it subconsciously, without perceptible effort. The surpassing skill of his tracking did not strike me forcibly at first, for I can read an open trail as well as the average cowman, and the mark of their passing lay plain before us; the veriest pilgrim, new come from graded roads and fenced pastures, could have counted the number of their steps—each hoof had stamped its impression in the soft loam as clearly as a steel die-cut in soaked leather. But that was where they had ridden while the land was still plastic from the rain. Farther, wind and sun had dried the ridge-turf to its normal firmness and baked the dobe flats till in places they were of their old flinty hardness. Yet Piegan crossed at a lope places where neither MacRae nor I could glimpse a sign—and when we would come again to soft ground the trail of the three would rise up to confront us, and bid us marvel at the keenness of his vision. He had a gift that we lacked.

We followed in the wake of Piegan Smith with what speed the coulée-gashed prairie permitted, and about three o'clock halted for half an hour to let our horses graze; we had been riding steadily over four hours, and it behooved us to have some thought for our mounts. Within ten minutes of starting again we dipped into a wide-bottomed coulée and came on the place where the three had made their first night-camp—a patch of dead ashes, a few half-burned sticks, and the close-cropped grass-plots where each horse had circled a picket-pin.

Beyond these obvious signs, there was nothing to see. Nothing, at least, that I could see except faint tracks leading away from the spot. These we had followed but a short distance when Piegan, who was scrutinizing the ground with more care than he had before shown, pulled up with an exclamation.

"Blamed if they ain't got company, from the look uh things," he grunted, squinting down. "I thought that was considerable of a trail for them t' make. You fellers wait here a minute. I want t' find out which way them tracks come in."

He loped back, swinging in north of the campground. While he was gone, MacRae and I leaned over in our saddles and scanned closely the grass-carpeted bottom-land. That the hoofs of passing horses had pressed down the rank growth of grass was plain enough, but whether the hoofs of six or a dozen we could only guess. Piegan turned, rode to where they had built their fire, circled the place, then came back to us.

"All right," he said. "I was sure there was more livestock left that campin'-place than we followed in. They come from the north—four hosses, two uh them rode an' the other two led, I think, from the way they heaved around a-crossin' a washout back yonder."

A mile or so farther we crossed a bare sandy stretch on the flat bottom of another coulée, and on its receptive surface the trail lay like a printed page—nine distinct, separate horse-tracks.

"Five riders an' four extra hosses, if I ain't read the sign wrong," Piegan casually remarked. "Say, we'll have our hands full if we bump into this bunch unexpected, eh?"

"They'll make short work of us if they get half a chance," Mac agreed. "But we'll make it a surprise party if we can."

From there on Piegan set a pace that taxed our horses' mettle—that was one consolation—we were well mounted. All three of us were good for a straightaway chase of a hundred miles if it came to a showdown. Piegan knew that we must do our trailing in daylight, and rode accordingly. He kept their trail with little effort, head cocked on one side like a saucy meadowlark, and whistled snatches of "Hell Among the Yearlin's," as though the prospect of a sanguinary brush with thieves was pleasing in the extreme.

The afternoon was on its last lap when we came in sight of Stony Crossing. The trail we followed wound along the crest of a ridge midway between the Crossing and Ten Mile Spring, where we had left Baker's outfit that rainy morning. The freighters had moved camp, but the mud and high water had held them, for we could see the white-sheeted wagons and a blur of cattle by the cottonwood grove where Hank Rowan had made his last stand. Presently we crossed the trail made by the string of wagons; it was fresh; made that morning, I judged. A little farther, on a line between the Crossing and the Spring, Piegan pulled up again, and this time the cause of his halting needed no explanation. The bunch had stopped and tarried there a few minutes, as the jumbled hoof-marks bore witness, and the track of two horses led away toward Ten Mile Spring.

"Darn it all!" Piegan grumbled. "Now, what d'yuh reckon's the meanin' uh that? Them two has lit straight for where Baker's layout was camped this mornin'. What for? Are they pullin' out uh the country with the coin? Or are they lookin' for you fellers?"

"Well"—MacRae thought a moment—"considering the care they've taken to cover up their movements, I don't see what other object they could have in view but making a smooth getaway. They've worked it nicely all around. You know that if there was anything they wanted they weren't taking any risk by going to any freight camp. We're the only men in the country that know why they are pulling out this way—and *they* know that we daren't go in and report it, because they've managed to put us on the dodge. They have reason to be sure that headquarters wouldn't for a minute listen to a yarn like we'd have to tell—they'd have time to ride to Mexico, while we sucked our thumbs in the guardhouse waiting for the rest of the Police to get wise by degrees."

"Then I tell yuh what let's do," Piegan abruptly decided. "I like t' know what's liable t' happen when I'm on a jaunt uh this kind. One of us better head in for the Crossin' an' find out for sure if any uh them fellers come t' the camp, an' what he wanted there. An' seein' nobody outside uh Horner knows I'm in on this play, I reckon I better go m'self. If there should happen t' be a stray trooper hangin' round there, the same would be mighty awkward for you fellers. So I'll go. You poke along the trail slow, an' I'll overhaul yuh."

"All right," MacRae agreed, and Piegan forthwith departed for the Crossing.

After Piegan left us we rode at a walk, and even then it was something of a task to follow the faint impression. In the course of an hour a cluster of dark objects appeared on the bench, coming rapidly toward us. MacRae brought the glasses to bear on them at once, for there was always the unpleasant possibility of Mounted Policemen cutting in on our trail; the riders of every post along the line were undoubtedly on the watch for us.

"It's Piegan and another fellow," Mac announced shortly. "They're leading two extra horses, and Piegan has changed mounts himself. I wonder what's up—they seem to be in a dickens of a hurry."

We got off and waited for them, wondering what the change of horses might portend. They swung down to us on a run, and it needed no second glance at the features of Piegan Smith to know that he brought with him a fresh supply of trouble. His scraggly beard was thrust forward aggressively, and his deep-set eyes fairly blazed between narrowed lids.

"Slap your saddles on them fresh hosses," he grated harshly from the back of a deep-chested, lean-flanked gray. "Let the others go—to hell if they want to!"

"What's up?" I asked sharply, and MacRae flung the same query over one shoulder as he fumbled at the tight-drawn latigo-knot.

Piegan rose in his stirrups and raised a clenched fist; the seamed face of him grew purple under its tan, and the words came out like the challenge of a range-bull.

"Them—them —— —— —— —— —— has got your girl!" he roared.

The latigo dropped from MacRae's hand. "What?" he turned on Piegan savagely, incredulously.

"I said it—I said it! Yuh heard me, didn't yuh!" Piegan shouted. "This mornin' about sunrise. That Hicks—the damned —— —— — — he come t' Baker's as they hooked up t' leave the Spring. He had a note for her, an' she dropped everything an' jumped on a hoss he'd brought an' rode away with him, cryin' when she left. He told Horner you'd bin shot resistin' arrest, an' wanted t' see her afore yuh cashed in. They ain't seen hide nor hair uh her since. Aw, don't stand starin' at me thataway. Hurry up! They ain't got twelve hours' start—an' by God I'll smell 'em out in the dark for this!"

It was like a knife-thrust in the back; such a devilish and unexpected turn of affairs that for half a second I had the same shuddery feeling that came to me the night I stooped over Hans Rutter and gasped at sight of what the fiends had done. MacRae whitened, but the full import of Piegan's words stunned him to silence. The bare possibility of Lyn Rowan being at the dubious mercy of those ruthless brutes was something that called for more than mere words. He hesitated only a moment, nervously twisting the saddle-strings with one hand, then straightened up and tore loose the cinch fastening.

After that outburst of Piegan's no one spoke. While Mac and I transferred our saddles to the Baker horses, Piegan swung down from his gray and, opening the pack on the horse we had been leading, took out a little bundle of flour and bacon and coffee and tied it behind the cantle of his saddle. A frying-pan and coffee-pot he tossed to me. Then we mounted and took to the trail again, stripped down to fighting-trim, unhampered by a pack-horse.

Of daylight there yet remained a scant two hours in which we could hope to distinguish a hoof-mark. Piegan leaned over his saddle-horn and took hills and hollows, wherever the trail led, with a rush that unrolled the miles behind us at a marvelous rate. For an hour we galloped silently, matching the speed of fresh, wiry horses against the dying day, no sound arising in that wilderness of brown coulée banks and dun-colored prairie but the steady beat of hoofs, and the purr of a rising breeze from the east. Then I became aware that Piegan, watching the ground through half-closed eyelids, was speaking to us. From riding a little behind, to give him room to trail, we urged our horses alongside.

"Them fellers at Baker's camp," he said, without looking up, "would 'a' come in a holy minute if there'd been hosses for 'em t' ride. But they only had enough saddle-stock along t' wrangle the bulls—an' I took three uh the best they had. Three of us is enough, anyhow. We kain't ride up on them fellers now an' go t' shootin'. They're all together again. I seen, back a ways, where them two hoss-tracks angled back from the spring. They must 'a' laid up at that camp we passed till sometime before daylight—seein' that damned Hicks come t' Baker's early this mornin'. An' if they didn't travel very fast t'-day—which ain't likely, 'cause they probably figure they're dead safe, and their track don't show a fast gait—there's just a chance that we'll hit 'em by dark if we burn the earth. We're good for thirty miles before night covers up their track. Don't yuh worry none, old boy," he bellowed at MacRae. "Old Injun Smith'll see yuh through. God! I could 'a' cried m'self when I hit that camp an' the old nigger woman went t' bawlin' when I told her yuh was both out on the bench, sound as a new dollar. That was the first they suspicioned anythin' was wrong. Them dirty, low-lived —— —— ——!"

Piegan lapsed into a string of curses. MacRae, apparently unmoved, nodded comprehension. But I knew what he was thinking, and I knew that when once we got within striking distance of Hicks, Gregory & Co., there would be new faces in hell without delay.

We slowed our horses to a walk to ascend an abrupt ridge. When we gained the top a vast stretch of the Northwest spread away to the east and north. Piegan lifted his eyes from the trail for an instant.

"Great Lord!" he said. "Look at the buffalo. It'll be good-by t' these tracks before long."

As far as the eye could reach the prairie was speckled with the herds, speckled with groups of buffalo as the sky is dotted with clusters of bright stars on a clear night. They moved, drifting slowly, in a southerly direction, here in sharply defined groups, there in long lines, farther in indistinct masses. But they moved; and the air that filled our nostrils was freighted with the tang of smoke.

We did not halt on the ridge. There was no need. We knew without speculating what the buffalo-drift and the smoke-tinged air presaged; and it bade us make haste before the tracks were quite obliterated.

So with the hill behind us, and each of us keeping his thoughts to himself—none of them wholly pleasant, judging by my own—we galloped down the long slope, a red sunset at our backs and in our faces a gale of dry, warm wind, tainted with the smell of burning grass. And at the bottom of the slope, in the depths of a high-walled coulée where the evening shadows were mustering for their stealthy raid on the gilded uplands, we circled a grove of rustling poplars and jerked our horses up short at sight of a scarlet blotch among the gloom of the trees.

CHAPTER XVIII.

HONOR AMONG THIEVES.

We knew, even as our fingers instinctively closed on the handles of our six-shooters, that we had not come upon the men we wanted; in such a case there would have been an exchange of leaden courtesies long before we managed to get in their immediate vicinity. It was unlikely that they would cease to exercise the cunning and watchfulness that had, so far, carried their infernal schemes through with flying colors. And a second look showed us that the scarlet coat belonged to a man who half-sat, half-lay on the ground, his shoulders braced against the trunk of a fallen tree. We got off our horses and went cautiously up to him.

"Be not afraid; it is only I!" Goodell raised his head with an effort and greeted us mockingly. "I am, as you can see, hors de combat. What is your pleasure, gentlemen?"

The weakness of his tone and the pallid features of him vouched for the truth of his statement. Stepping nearer, we saw that the light-colored shirt showing between the open lapels of his jacket was stained a tell-tale crimson. The hand he held against his breast was dabbled and streaked with the blood that oozed from beneath the pressing fingers; the leaf-mold under him was saturated with it.

"Where is the rest of the bunch?" MacRae asked him evenly. "You seem to have got a part of what is coming to you, but your skirts aren't clear, for all that."

"You have a bone to pick with me, eh?" Goodell murmured. "Well, I don't blame you. But don't adopt the role of inquisitor—because I'm as good as dead, and dead men tell no tales. My mouth will be closed forever in a little while—and I can die as easily with it unopened. But if you'll get me a drink of water, and be decent about it, I'll unfold a tale that's worth while. I assure you it will be to your interest to give me a hearing."

Piegan turned and strode out of the timber. He unfastened the coffee-pot from my saddle, and made for the coulée channel we had crossed, in which a buffalo-wallow still held water from the recent rain.

Goodell coughed, and a red, frothy stream came from his lips. It isn't in the average man to be utterly callous to the suffering of another, even if that other richly deserves his pain. Notwithstanding the deviltry he and his confederates had perpetrated, I couldn't help feeling sorry for Goodell—what little I'd seen of him had been likable enough. I found it hard to look at him there and believe him guilty of murder, robbery, and kindred depredations. He was beyond reach of earthly justice, anyway; and one can't help forgiving much to a man who faces death with a smile.

"Are you in any pain, Goodell?" I asked.

"None whatever," he answered weakly. "But I'm a goner, for all that. I have a very neat knife-thrust in the back. Also a bullet somewhere in my lungs. You see in me," he drawled, "a victim of chivalry. I've played for big stakes; I've robbed gaily, and killed a man or two in the way of fighting; all of which sits lightly on my conscience. But there are two things I haven't done. I want you to remember distinctly that I have *not* dragged that girl into this—nor had any hand in torturing a wounded old man."

"You mean Lyn Rowan? Is she safe?" Mac squatted beside him, leaning eagerly forward to catch the reply. Piegan returned with the water as Goodell was about to answer. He swallowed thirstily, took breath, and went on.

"Yes, I mean her," he said huskily. "I'll tell you quick, for I know I won't last long, and when I'm done you'll know where to look for them. I started this thing—this hold-up business—no matter why. Lessard was away in the hole—gambling and other things—I hinted the idea to him; he jumped at it, as I thought he would. And——"

"Lessard!" I interrupted. "He was in on this, then?"

"Was he?" Goodell echoed. "He is the whole thing."

I had suspected as much, but sometimes it is a surprise to have one's suspicions confirmed. I glanced at Mac and Piegan.

"I was sure of it all along," Mac answered my unspoken thought. Piegan merely shrugged his shoulders.

"I wanted to get that government money in the pay-wagon, that was all—at first," Goodell continued. "We planned a long time ahead, and we had to take in those three to make it go. Then Lessard found out about those two old miners, and put Hicks and Gregory on their trail unknown to me—I had no hand in that foul business. You know the result—the finish—that night you lost the ten thousand—it was hellish work. I wanted to kill Hicks and Gregory when they told me. Poor old Dutchman! Lessard put Bevans on your trail, Flood. He followed you from Walsh that day, and you played into his hands that night when you stirred up the fire. Only for running into his partners, he would probably have murdered you for that ten thousand some night while you slept. Give me another drink."

I lifted the pot of water to his lips again, and he thanked me courteously.

"Then Lessard conceived the theory that you fellows had learned more than you told. We were fixed to get the paymaster on that trip. We shook you, and did the job. MacRae was on the way—you know. He sent you to the Stone with those devils to keep cases on you. It seemed a pity to let slip that gold-dust after they had gone so far. You know how that panned out. We had a stake then. Lessard was the brains, the guiding genius; we did the work. The original plan was to make a clean-up, divide with him, and get out of the country—while he used his authority to throw the Force off the track till we were well away. Then the girl appeared, and Lessard lost his head. She turned him down; and at the last moment he upset our plans by deciding to cut loose and go with us. I believe now that he hatched this latest scheme when she refused him. I tell you he was fairly mad about her. He took advantage of this last trip to loot the post of all the funds he could lay hands on. We have—or, rather, *they* have," he corrected, "about a hundred and fifty thousand altogether.

"We couldn't ford Milk River on account of the storm. You tracked us? You saw our last camp? Yes. Well, we left there early this morning. And when Hicks turned off opposite Baker's outfit with an extra horse, I thought nothing of it—it was perfectly safe, and we needed more matches, Lessard said. Not until he joined us later with the girl did I suspect that there were wheels within wheels; a kidnapping had never occurred to me; I hadn't thought his infatuation would carry him that far. She realized at once that she had been hoodwinked, and appealed to Lessard. He laughed at her, and told her that he had abandoned the modern method of winning a mate, and gone back to the primitive mode.

"I've put myself beyond the pale; outlaw, thief, what you like—I'm not sensitive to harsh names. But a woman—a good woman! Well, I have my own ideas about such things. And when we camped here, I had made up my mind. I told Lessard she must go back. That was a foolish move. I should have got the drop and killed him out of hand. While I argued with him, Hicks slipped a knife into my back, and as I turned on him Lessard shot me. Ah, well—it'll be all the same a hundred years from now. But I'd like to put a spoke in their wheel for the sake of that blue-eyed girl.

"MacRae, you and Smith know the mouth of Sage Creek, and the ford there. That's where they'll camp to-night. I doubt if they'll cross the river till morning. If you ride you can make it in three hours. From there they plan to follow Milk River to the Missouri and catch a down-stream boat. But you'll get them to-night. You must. Now give me another drink—and drift!"

"We'll get them, Goodell." MacRae rose to his feet as he spoke. "You're white, if you did get off wrong. I'll remember what you did—for her. Is there anything we can do for you?"

Goodell shook his head. "I tell you," he said, and turned his head to look wistfully up at the eastern coulée-rim, all tinted with the blazing sunset. "I'll go out over the hills with the shadows. An hour—maybe two. It's my time. I've no complaint to make. All I want is a drink. You can do no good for a dead man; and the living are sorely in need. It'll be a bit lonesome, that's all."

"No message for anybody?" MacRae persisted.

"No—yes!" The old mocking, reckless tone crept into his voice again. "If you should have speech with Lessard before you put his light out, tell him I go to prepare a place for him—a superheated grid! Now drift—*vamos*—hit the trail. Remember, the gorge at the mouth of Sage Creek. Good-by."

Soberly we filed out from among the trees, now swaying in the grip of the wind, their leafy boughs rustling sibilantly; as though the weird sisters whispered in the nodding branches that here was another thread full-spun and ready for the keen shears. Soberly we swung to the saddle and rode slowly away, lest the quick beat of hoofs should bring a sudden pang of loneliness to the intrepid soul calmly awaiting death under the shivering trees. I think that one bold effort to right a wrong will more than wipe out the black score against him when the Book of Life is balanced.

A little way beyond the poplar-grove Piegan drew rein, and held up one hand.

"Poor devil," he muttered. "He's a-calling us."

But he wasn't. He was fighting off the chill of loneliness that comes to the strongest of us when we face the unknowable, the empty void that there is no escaping. Dying there in the falling dusk, he was singing to himself as an Indian brave chants his death-song when the red flame of the torture-fire bites into his flesh.

> Sing heigh, sing ho, for the Cavalier!
> Sing heigh, sing ho, for the Crown.
> Gentlemen all, turn out, turn out;
> We'll keep these Roundheads down!

Down—down—down—down.
We'll ke—ep these Round—heads down!

Once—twice, the chorus of that old English Royalist song rose up out of the grove. Then it died away, and we turned to go. And as we struck home the spurs, remembering the mouth of Sage Creek and the dark that was closing down, a six-shooter barked sharply, back among the trees.

I swung my horse around in his tracks and raced him back to the poplars, knowing what I would find, and yet refusing to believe. I will not say that his big heart had failed him; perhaps it did not seem to him worth while to face the somber shadows to the bitter end, lying alone in that deep hollow in the earth. It may be that the night looked long and comfortless, and it was his wish to go out with the sun. He lay beside the fallen tree, his eyes turned blankly to the darkening sky, the six-shooter in his hand as he had held it for the last time. I straightened his arms, and covered his face with the blood-stained coat and left him to his long sleep. And even old Piegan lifted his hat and murmured "Amen" in all sincerity as we turned away.

CHAPTER XIX.

THE BISON.

When we reached high ground again the twilight was fading to a semicircle of bloodshot gray in the northwest. The wind still blew squarely in our faces. Down in the coulée we had not noticed it so much, but now every breath was rank with the smell of grass-smoke, and each mile we traversed the stink of it grew stronger.

"We'll be blamed lucky if we don't run into a prairie-fire before mornin'," Piegan grumbled. "If that wind don't let up, she'll come a-whoopin'. It'll be a sure enough smoky one, too, with this mixture uh dry grass an' the new growth springin' up. It didn't rain so hard down in this country, I notice. Ain't that a lalla of a smell?"

Neither of us answered, and Piegan said no more. It grew dark—dark in the full sense of the word. The smoke-burdened atmosphere was impervious to the radiance of the stars. Only by Smith's instinctive sense of direction did we make any headway toward the mouth of Sage Creek. Even MacRae owned himself somewhat at fault, once we came among the buffalo. They barred our path in dimly-seen masses that neither halted, scattered, nor turned aside when we galloped upon them in the gloom. We were the ones who gave the road, riding now before, now behind the indistinct bulk of a herd, according as we judged the shorter way.

More dense became the brute mass. Whirled this way and that, as Piegan led, I knew neither east, west, north or south from one moment to another. Betimes we found a stretch of open country, and gave our horses the steel, but always to bring up suddenly against the bison plodding in groups, in ranks, in endless files. They were ubiquitous; stolid obstructions that we could neither avoid nor ride down. Our progress became monotonous, a succession of fruitless attempts to advance; hopeless, like wandering in a subtle maze. Bison to the right of us, bison to the left of us, an uncounted swarm behind us, and as many before—but they neither bellowed nor thundered; they passed like phantoms in the night, soundlessly save for the muffled trampling of cloven hoofs, and here and there upon occasion hoarse coughings that were strangled by the wind.

And we rode as silently as the bison marched. For each one of us had seen that one-minded pilgrimage of the brown cattle take place in moons gone by. I recalled a time when a trail-herd lay on the Platte and the buffalo barred their passing for two days—even made fourteen riders and three thousand Texas steers give ground. Is it not history that the St. Louis-Benton river-boats backed water when the bison crossed the Missouri in the spring and fall? Remembering these, and other times that the herds had gathered and swept over the plains, a plague of monstrous locusts, pushing aside men and freight-trains, I knew what would happen should the buffalo close their ranks, marshal the scattered groups into closer formation, quicken the pace of the multitude that poured down from the north. And presently it happened.

Insensibly the number of moving bodies increased. The consolidation was imperceptible in the murk, but nevertheless it took place. We ceased to find clear spaces where we could gallop; a trot became impossible. We were hemmed in. A rank animal odor mingled with the taint of smoke. Gradually the muffled beat of hoofs grew more pronounced, a shuffling monotone that filled the night. We were mere atoms in a vast wave of horn and bone and flesh that bore us onward as the tide floats driftwood.

The belated moon stole up from its lair, hovered above the sky-line, a gaudy orange sphere in the haze of smoke. It shed a tenuous glimmer on the sea of bison that had engulfed us; and at the half-revealed sight MacRae lifted his clenched hands above his head and cursed the circumstance that had brought us to such extremity. That was the first and only time I knew him to lose his poise, his natural repression. Still water runs deep, they say; and a glacial cap may conceal subterranean fires. Trite similes, I grant you—but, ah, how true. The good Lord help those phlegmatics who can stand by unmoved when a self-contained man reveals the anguish of his soul in one passionate outburst. Could the fury that quivered in his voice have wreaked itself on the bison and the men we followed, the stench of their blasted carcasses would have reached high heaven. But the bison surrounded us impassively, bore us on as before; somewhere, miles beyond, Lessard pursued the evil tenor of his way; and MacRae's futile passion, like a wave that has battered itself to foam against a sullen cliff, subsided and died. Later, while we three cast-aways drifted with the bovine tide, he spoke to Piegan Smith.

A WAR FOR THE OPEN ROAD AGAINST AN ENEMY
WHOSE ONLY WEAPON WAS HIS UNSWERVING BULK.

"How are we going to get through?"

"Dunno. But we *will* get through, yuh c'n gamble on that." Optimism rampant was the dominating element in Piegan's philosophy of life.

As if to prove that he was a true prophet, the herd split against a rocky pinnacle, and on this we stranded. So much, at least, we had gained—we were no longer being carried willy-nilly out of our way.

"If they'd only scatter a little," MacRae muttered.

But for a long two hours the bison streamed by our island, dividing before and closing behind the insensate peak that alone had power to break their close-packed ranks. Then came an opening, a falling apart; slight as it was, we plunged into it with joy. Thereafter we were buffeted like chips in the swirling maw of a whirlpool; we fought our way rod by rod. Here an opening, and we shot through; there a solid wall of flesh for whose passing we halted, lashing out with quirts and spurring desperately to hold our own—a war for the open road against an enemy whose only weapon was his unswerving bulk. And we won. We pushed, twisted, spurred our way through the ranks of a hundred thousand bison. Jostling, cursing the brute swarm, we crowded our horses against the press, and lo! of a sudden we reined up on open ground—the bison, like a nightmare, were gone. Off in the gloom to one side of us a myriad of hoofs beat the earth, the hoarse coughings continued, the animal odor exhaled—but it was no longer a force to be reckoned with. We were free. We had outflanked the herd.

CHAPTER XX.

THE MOUTH OF SAGE CREEK.

With that opposing force behind us, we bore away across the shrouded benches, straight for the mouth of Sage Creek. What method we would pursue when we got there was not altogether clear to me, and the same thing evidently bothered Piegan, for, after a long interval, he addressed himself pointedly to MacRae.

"We ought t' hit the river in an hour or so," he said. "It's time we figured on how we're goin' t' work, eh? I wish t' the Lord it was daylight."

"So do I," MacRae moodily responded. "For that matter, it won't be long. I've been thinking that the best way would be to get down on the flat at the north of the creek and *cache* our horses in the timber. Then we can sneak around without making any noise. If they're not camped on the flat, we'll find them somewhere up the gorge. Of course, there's a chance that they have crossed the river—but if they didn't get there in daylight, and the river is still high, I hardly think they'd risk fording in the dark."

"That's about the way I had sized it up," Piegan replied. "The flat ain't bigger'n a good-sized flapjack, nohow, an' if they're on that or up in Sage Creek canyon, we're bound t' locate 'em; kain't help hearin' their hosses snort or cough or make some sort uh noise, if we go careful. The worst of it is, we kain't start the ball a-rollin' till we get that girl spotted—that's the hell of it! Like as not she'd be the first one t' get hurt. An' if we get rambunctious an' stir 'em up in the dark, an' *don't* put the finishin' to 'em right then an' there—why, they got all the show in the world t' make a hot-foot getaway. *Sabe?* While I ain't lookin' for a chance t' sidestep the game, for I know how yuh feel, I'd say locate 'em if we can, an' then back up a little and wait for day."

"Oh, I know, I know!" Mac burst out. "That's sense. But it gives me the creeps to think—to think——"

"Sure; we know it," Piegan answered softly. "We kain't tell till we get there, anyway. Maybe we'll get 'em dead t' rights. No tellin' what'll come up when we get into that canyon. When we get 'em spotted we c'n make up our minds what t' do—if we have any time t' talk about it," he finished, in an undertone.

As we rode, the crimson-yellow reflection of burning prairies began to tint the eastern sky; once, from the crest of a hill, we saw the wavering line of flame, rising and falling in beautiful undulations. And presently we galloped across a mile or two of level grassland and pulled up on the very brink of Sage Creek canyon.

"Easy, easy, from here on," Piegan whispered caution. "We may be right above 'em, for all we know. We hit it a little too high up. How far d'yuh reckon it is t' the mouth, Mac?"

"Not more than half a mile," MacRae returned. "We're not far out. I know where there's a good place to get down."

We turned sharply to the right, coming out on a narrow point. Without mishap we reached the foot of the steep hill. At the bottom the wind was almost wholly shut off, so that sounds were easier to distinguish. The moon had passed its zenith long since, and half of the flat lay in dense shadow. Beyond the shadow a pall of smoke lay over everything, a shifting haze that made objects near at hand indefinite of outline, impossible to classify at a glance. A horse or a tree or a clump of brush loomed up grotesquely in the vaporous blur.

Mac, to whom the topography of that gloomy place was perfectly familiar, led the way. A black, menacing wall that rose before us suddenly resolved itself into a grove of trees, great four-foot cottonwoods. He stole into the heart of the grove and satisfied himself that our game had not appropriated it as a camping-place. That assured, we followed with our horses and tied them securely, removing saddles and bridles, lest the clank of steel or creaking of leather betray our presence to listening ears. On any noise our horses might make we had no choice but to take a chance. Then we looked to our guns and set out on a stealthy search.

A complete circle of that tiny bottom—it was only a shelf of sage-brown land lying between the river and the steep bank—profited us nothing, and Piegan whispered that now we must seek for them in the gorge.

Cautiously we retraced our steps from the lower end of the flat, and turned into the narrow mouth of the canyon. We had no more than got fairly between the straight-up-and-down walls of it than Piegan halted us with a warning hand. We squatted in the sage-brush and listened. Behind us, from the river, came a gentle plashing.

"Beaver," I hazarded.

"Too loud," Piegan murmured. "Let's go back an' see."

We reached the river-edge just in time to hear the splashing die away; and though we strained our eyes looking, we could make out no movement on the surface of the river or in the dimly-outlined scrub that fringed the opposite bank. Piegan turned on the instant and ran to where we had tied our horses; but they stood quietly as we had left them.

"I got a hunch they'd got onto us, an' maybe set us afoot for a starter," Piegan explained. "I reckon that must 'a' been a deer or some other wild critter."

Once more we turned into the canyon, and this time followed its narrow, scrub-patched floor some three hundred yards up from the river. It was dark enough for any kind of deviltry in that four-hundred foot gash in the earth; the sinking moon lightened only a strip along the east wall, near the top; lower down, smoke mingling with the natural gloom cast an impenetrable veil from bank to bank; not a breath of air stirred the tomblike stillness. Directly in front of us a horse coughed. We dropped on all fours, listened a moment, then crept forward. Without warning, we found ourselves foul of a picket-line, and the vague forms of grazing horses loomed close by. Piegan halted us with a touch, and we lay flat; then with our heads together he whispered softly:

"We must be right on top uh them. It's a cinch their camp ain't far from their livestock. I wonder— —"

To the left of us a horse snorted nervously; we heard him trot with high, springy strides to the end of his rope, and snort again. Then a voice cut the stillness that followed: "Here, you fool, what's the matter with you?"

We hugged the ground like frightened rabbits. It hardly seemed possible that we could be within speaking-distance of them—yet that was Gregory's clear enunciation; I would know his speech in a jabberfest of several nations.

"What's the matter?" That, by the curt inflection, the autocratic peremptoriness, was Lessard. I had one hand on MacRae's shoulder, and I felt a tremor run through his body, like the rising of a cat's fur at sight of an adversary.

"Oh, nothing much," Gregory answered carelessly. "I was just speaking to one of these fool horses. They seem to be as nervous as you are." And we could hear him chuckle over this last remark.

After that there was nothing but the muffled tr-*up*, tr-*up* of grazing horses. Piegan or MacRae, I could not tell which, tugged gently at my arm, and the three of us retreated slowly, crawling both literally and figuratively. When we were well away from the camp of that ungodly combination, Piegan rose to his feet and we proceeded a little faster until we reached a distance that permitted of low-toned conversation.

"Now," Piegan declared, "we have 'em located. An' I'm here t' declare that it's plumb foolish t' mix things with that layout till we can see t' shoot tolerable straight. If we go against 'em now, it'll be all same goin' blindfolded into a barn t' pick out the best hoss. The first gun that pops they'll raise up an' quit the earth like a bunch uh antelope. *They* ain't got nothin' t' win in a fight—unless they're cornered. I did think uh tryin' t' get off with their hosses, but I figured it wouldn't pay with that sharp-eared cuss on the watch. Whenever it comes day, we got all the best uh things—though I don't reckon we'll have a walkaway. We want t' make a clean job once we start in, an' we kain't do that in the dark. Furthermore, as I said before, if we go t' throwin' lead when we kain't see ten feet in front of us, we'd just about hit that girl first rattle out uh the box. She ain't comin' t' no harm just now, or it wouldn't be so blamed peaceful around there. It's only a matter of a couple uh hours t' daylight, anyhow. What d'yuh think?"

"Under the circumstances, the only thing we can do is to wait," MacRae assented, and I fancied that there was a reluctant quiver in his usually steady voice. "It's going to be smoky at daybreak, but we can see their camp from this first point, I think. There's a big rock over here—I'll show you—you and Sarge can get under cover there. I'll lie up on the opposite side, so they'll have to come between us. Let them pack and get started. When they get nearly abreast, cut loose. Shoot their saddle-horses first, then we can fight it out. Come on, I'll show you that rock."

MacRae's bump of location was nearly as well developed as Piegan's. He picked his way through the sage-brush to the other side of the canyon, bringing us in the deepest gloom to a great slab of sandstone that had fallen from above, and lay a few feet from the base of the sheer wall. It was a natural breastwork, all ready to our hand. There, without another word, he left us. Crouching in the shelter of that rock, not daring to speak above a whisper, denied the comforts of tobacco, it seemed as if we were never to be released from the dusky embrace of night. In reality it was less than two hours till daybreak, but they were slow-footed ones to me. Then dawn flung itself impetuously across the hills, and the naked rim of the canyon took form in a shifting whirl of smoke. Down in the depths gloom and shadows vanished together, and Piegan Smith

and I peered over the top of our rock and saw the outlaw camp—
men and horses dim figures in the growing light. We scanned the
opposite side for sight of MacRae, but saw nothing of him; he kept
close under cover.

"They're packin' up," Piegan murmured, with a dry chuckle. "I
reckon things won't tighten nor nothin' in a few minutes, eh? But
say, damn if I see anything among that layout that resembles a
female. Do you?"

I did not, even when I focused the field-glasses on that bunch at that
short distance. Certainly she was not there—at least she was not to
be seen, and I could almost read the expression on each man's
features, so close did the glasses draw them up. And failing to see
her started me thinking that after all she might have given them the
slip. I hoped it might be so. Lyn was no chicken-hearted weakling, to
sit down and weep unavailingly in time of peril. Bred on the range,
on speaking-terms with the turbulent frontier life, her wits weren't
likely to forsake her in a situation of that kind.

While the light of day grew stronger and the smoke eddied in
heavier wreaths above, one of them swung up on a horse and came
down the bottom at a fast lope. We had no means of knowing what
his mission might be, but I did know that the square shoulders, the
lean eagle face, could only belong to one man; and I dropped the
glasses and drew a bead on his breast. I hesitated a second, squinting
along the barrel of the carbine; I wanted him to round the point that
jutted out from the other side of the canyon, so that his partners
could not see his finish. If they did not see him go down, nor observe
the puff of smoke from behind the rock, they might think he had
fired a shot himself. And while I waited, grumbling at the
combination of circumstances that made it necessary to shoot down
even a cold-blooded brute like him in such a way, Mac took the
matter out of my hands in his own characteristic fashion.

Lessard turned the point, and as the carbine-hammer clicked back
under the pull of my thumb, MacRae sprang to his feet from behind
a squatty clump of sage, right in Lessard's path. Nervy as men are

made, MacRae worshiped at the shrine of an even break, a square deal for friend or foe. And Lessard got it. There among the sagebrush he got a fair chance for his life, according to the code of men who settle their differences at the business end of a six-shooter. But it wasn't Lessard's hour. Piegan Smith and I saw his hand flash to his pistol, saw it come to a level, heard the single report of MacRae's gun. It was a square deal—which Lessard had not given us. He crumpled in the saddle; sprawled a moment on the neck of his horse, and dropped to the ground. MacRae sank behind the sage again, and we waited for the others.

CHAPTER XXI.

AN ELEMENTAL ALLY.

But they did not come. One of them must have seen Lessard fall, for at the crack of MacRae's gun men and horses, already half-hidden by the thickening smoke, vanished into the brush. Piegan fired one ineffectual shot as they flicked out of sight. So far we had seen nothing of Lyn. I was satisfied she was not in the party, unaccountable as that seemed to be.

"Darn 'em," Piegan grunted disgustedly. "They're next, now. An' they don't aim t' run the gantlet till they have t'. We got 'em penned, anyway; they can't get out uh that patch uh brush without showin' themselves."

"Oh, Piegan!" MacRae called to us. He lay within easy shouting-distance, and managed to make himself heard without rising.

"Hello!" Piegan answered.

"Can you fellows keep them from going up the canyon?"

"I reckon we can," Smith called back, "unless this smoke gets so blame thick we kain't see at all."

"All right. I'm going up on top, and throw it into them from above. Maybe I can drive them out of the brush."

Piegan slapped me on the shoulder. "Darn our fool hearts," he exclaimed. "We ought to 'a' thought uh that before. Why, he c'n pick 'em off like blackbirds on a fence, from up there on the bench!"

We did not see MacRae go, but we knew that he must have crawled through the sage-brush to the creek channel, where, by stooping, he could gain the mouth of the canyon unseen. Anyway, our time was fully occupied in watching the brush-patch that sheltered our plundering friends. They held close to their concealment, however, nor did they waste any powder on us—for that matter, I don't think they knew just where we were, and they were familiar enough with the gentle art of bushwhacking to realize that the open was a distinctly unhealthy place for either party to prospect.

It was a long time till we heard from MacRae again, and, lying there passively, we grew afraid that after all they would give us the slip; for the smoke was now rolling in black clouds above the gorge. So far the thickest of it had blown overhead, but any moment a change of wind might whip it down the canyon bottom like an ocean fog, and that would mean good-by to Hicks & Co.

"That fire's mighty close, an' comin' on the jump," Piegan remarked, with an upward glance. "I wish she'd let up long enough for us t' finish this job. That smoke's as good as they want, once it begins t' settle in the gorge. What in thunder d'yuh s'pose Mac's doin' all this time. He ought t' show pretty quick, now."

He showed, as Piegan put it, very shortly. From the top of the opposite bank he fired a shot or two, and drew for the first time a return from the enemy. Then he broke off, and when he next gave hint of his whereabouts, it was to hail us from the nearest point on the canyon rim.

"Quit your hide-out and pull for the mouth of the gorge. Quick! I'll be there."

"What the hell's up now!" Piegan muttered. "Well, I guess we'll have t' take a chance. If they don't wing us before we get across this bald place, we'll be all right. Run like yuh was plumb scairt t' death, Flood."

We sprinted like a pair of quarter-horses across the thirty yards of bare ground that spread in front of the rock, a narrow enough space, to be sure, but barren of cover for a jack-rabbit, much less two decent-sized men. My heart was pumping double-quick when we threw ourselves headlong in the welcome sage-brush—they had done their level best to stop us, and some of those forty-four caliber humming-birds buzzed their leaden monotone perilously close to our heads. That is one kind of music for which I have a profound respect.

From there to the creek-channel we crawled on all fours, as MacRae had done. Stooping, lest our heads furnish a target, we splashed along in the shallow water till we reached the mouth of the canyon. There we slipped carefully to higher ground. MacRae was scrambling and sliding down from above, barely distinguishable against the bank. Far up the gorge dense clouds of black smoke swooped down from the benchland. Already the patch of brush in which lay the renegade Policemen was hidden in the smudge, shut away from our sight. We hailed MacRae when he reached the foot of the hill, and he came crashing through sage and buck-brush and threw himself, panting, on the ground.

"The fire," he gasped, "is coming down the gorge. They're cut off at the other end. They've got to come out here in a little while—or roast. The smoke would choke a salamander, on top, right now. We can't miss them in this narrow place, no matter how thick it gets. Look yonder!"

A wavering red line licked its way to the canyon-edge on the east side, wiped out the grass, and died on the bald rim-rock. Away up the creek a faint crackling sounded.

"Dry timber," Piegan muttered. "It'll get warm 'round here pretty directly."

The smoke, blacker now, more dense, hot as a whiff from a baker's oven, swooped down upon us in choking eddies. It blew out of the canyon-mouth like a gust from a chimney, rolling over and over in billowy masses. The banks on either hand were almost invisible. We knew that our time of waiting was short. The popping of dry, scrubby timber warned us that our position would soon be untenable. The infernal vapors from the unholy mixture of green and dry grass, berry bushes, willow scrub, and the ubiquitous sage, made breathing a misery and brought unwilling tears to our stinging eyes. And presently, above the subdued but menacing noises of the fire, the beat of galloping hoofs uprose.

They burst out of the mouth of the canyon, a smoke-wreathed whirlwind, heading for the protection of the river. The pack-horses, necked together, galloped in the lead, and behind them Hicks, Gregory, and Bevans leaned over the necks of their mounts. They knew that we were waiting for them, but at the worst they had a fighting chance with us, and none with what came behind. So thick hung the smoky veil that they were right on top of us before they took tangible shape; and when we rose to our knees and fired, the crack of their guns mingled with that of our own. Gregory, so near that I could see every feature of his dark face, the glittering black eyes, the wide mouth parted over white, even teeth, wilted in his saddle as they swept by. Bevans and his horse went down together. But Hicks the wily, a superb horseman, hung in his off stirrup and swerved away from us, and the smoke closed behind him to the tune of our guns.

It was done in less time than it has taken to tell of it. There was no prolonged hand-to-hand struggle with buckets of blood marring the surrounding scenery, and a beautiful heroine wringing her hands in despair; merely a rush of horses and men out of the smoke, a brief spasm of gun-fire—it was begun and ended in five seconds. But there were two fallen men, and Piegan Smith with a hole through the big muscle of his right arm, to show that we had fought.

The pack-horses, with no riders at their heels to guide them, had tangled each other in the connecting-rope and stopped. Hicks was gone, and likely to keep going. So we turned our attention to Gregory and Bevans. Gregory was dead as the proverbial door-nail, but Bevans, on investigation, proved to be very much alive—so much so that if he had not been partly stunned by the fall, and thereafter pinned to the ground by a thousand-pound horse, he would have potted one or two of us with a good heart. As it was, we reached the gentleman in the same moment that he made a heroic effort to lay hold of the carbine which had luckily—for us—fallen beyond the length of his arm.

"Yuh lay down there an' be good!" Piegan, out of the fullness of his heart, emphasized his command with the toe of his boot. "Where's that girl, yuh swine?"

"Go to hell!" Bevans snarled.

"Here," MacRae broke in hastily, "we've got to move pretty *pronto*, and get across the river. That fire will be on us in five minutes. Sarge and I will gather up their horses. You keep an eye on Bevans, Piegan; he'll answer questions fast enough when I get at him."

While Mac dashed across the creek I captured Gregory's horse, which had stopped when his rider fell; and as I laid hand on the reins I thought I heard a shot off beyond the river. But I couldn't be certain. The whine of the wind that comes with a fire, the crackle of the fire itself, the manifold sounds that echoed between the canyon walls and the pungent, suffocating smoke, all conspired against clear thinking or hearing. I listened a moment, but heard no more. Then, with time at a premium, I hastened to straighten out the tangle of pack-animals. Mac loomed up in the general blur with Lessard's body on his horse, as I led the others back to where Piegan stood guard over Bevans.

"Ain't this hell!" he coughed. "That fire's right on top of us. We got t' make the river in a hurry."

It was another minute's work to lash Gregory's body on one of the pack-horses, and release the sullen Bevans from the weight of his dead mount. As an afterthought, I looked in the pockets on his saddle, and the first thing I discovered was a wad of paper money big enough to choke an ox, as Piegan would say. I hadn't the time to investigate further, so I simply cut the *anqueros* off his saddle and flung them across the horn of my own—and even in that swirl of smoke and sparks I glowed with a sense of gratification, for it seemed that at last I was about to shake hands with the ten thousand dollars I had mourned as lost. Then Piegan and I drove Bevans ahead of us and moved the spoils of war to the river brink, while MacRae hurried to the cottonwood grove after our own neglected mounts; they had given us too good service to be abandoned to the holocaust.

MacRae soon joined us with the three horses; out into the stream, wading till the water gurgled around our waists, we led the bunch. Then we were compelled to take our hats and slosh water over packs and saddles till they were soaked—for the fire was ravaging the flat we had just left, and showers of tiny sparks descended upon and around us. Thus proof against the fiery baptism, though still half-strangled by the smoke, our breathing a succession of coughs, we mounted and pushed across.

The high water had abated and the river was now flowing at its normal stage, some three hundred yards in width and nowhere swimming-deep on the ford. We passed beyond spark-range and splashed out on a sand-bar that jutted from the southern bank. Midway between the lapping water and the brush that lined the edge of the flat, a dark object became visualized in the shifting gray vapor. We rode to it and pulled up in amaze. Patiently awaiting the pleasure of his master, as a good cavalry horse should, was the bay gelding Hicks had ridden; and Hicks himself sprawled in the sand at the end of the bridle-reins. I got down and looked him over. He was not dead; far from it. But a bullet had scored the side of his head above one ear, and he was down and out for the time.

We stripped the pistol-belt off him, and a knife. At the same time we rendered Bevans incapable of hostile movement by anchoring both hands securely behind his back with a pack-rope. That done, Piegan's bleeding arm came in for its share of attention. Then we held a council of war.

CHAPTER XXII.

SPEECHLESS HICKS.

When I spoke of holding a council of war, I did so largely in a figurative sense. Literally, we set about reviving Hicks, with a view to learning from him what had become of Lyn Rowan. He and Bevans undoubtedly knew, and as Bevans persisted in his defiant sullenness, refusing to open his mouth for other purpose than to curse us vigorously, we turned to Hicks. A liberal amount of water dashed in his face aided him to recover consciousness, and in a short time he sat up and favored us with a scowl.

"What has become of that girl you took away from Baker's freight-train yesterday morning?" MacRae dispassionately questioned.

Hicks glared at him by way of answer.

"Hurry up and find your tongue," MacRae prompted.

"I dunno what you're drivin' at," Hicks dissembled.

"You will know, in short order," MacRae retorted, "if you harp on that tune. We've got you where we want you, and I rather think you'll be glad to talk, before long. I ask you what became of that girl between the time you knifed Goodell and this morning?"

Hicks started at mention of Goodell. His heavy face settled into stubborn lines. He blinked under MacRae's steady look. Of a sudden he sprang to his feet. I do not know what his intention may have been, but he got little chance to carry out any desperate idea that took form in his brain, for MacRae knocked him back on his haunches with a single blow of his fist.

"Answer me," he shouted, "or by the Lord! I'll make you think hell is a pleasure-garden compared to this sand-bar."

"Kick a few uh his ribs out uh place for a starter," Piegan coolly advised. "That'll he'p him remember things."

Yet for all their threats Hicks obstinately refused to admit that he had ever seen Lyn Rowan. What his object was in denying knowledge we knew he possessed did not transpire till later. He knew the game was lost, so far as he was concerned, and he was mustering his forces in a last effort to save himself. And MacRae's patience snapped like a frayed thread before many minutes of futile query.

"Get me a rope off one of those pack-horses, Sarge," he snapped.

I brought the rope; and I will brazenly admit that I should not have balked at helping decorate the limb of a cottonwood with those two red-handed scoundrels. But I was not prepared for the turn MacRae took. Hicks evidently felt that there was something ominous to the fore, for he fought like a fiend when we endeavored to apply the rope to his arms and legs. There was an almost superhuman desperation in his resistance, and while MacRae and I hammered and choked him into submission Piegan gyrated about us with a gun in his left hand, begging us to let *him* put the finishing touches to Hicks. That, however, was the very antithesis of MacRae's purpose.

"I don't want to *kill* him, Piegan," he said pointedly, when Hicks was securely tied. "If I had, do you suppose I'd dirty my hands on him in that sort of a scramble when I know how to use a gun? I want him to talk—you understand?—and he *will* talk before I'm through with him."

There was a peculiar inflection about that last sentence, a world of meaning that was lost on me until I saw Mac go to the brush a few yards distant, return with an armful of dry willows and place them on the sand close by Hicks. Without audible comment I watched him, but I was puzzled—at first. He broke the dry sticks into fragments across his knee; when he had a fair-sized pile he took out his knife and whittled a few shavings. Not till he snapped his knife shut and put it in his pocket and began, none too gently, to remove the boots from Hicks' feet, did I really comprehend what he was about. It sent a shiver through me, and even old Piegan stood aghast at the malevolent determination of the man. But we voiced no protest. That was neither the time nor place to abide by the Golden Rule. Only the law of force, ruthless, inexorable, would compel speech from Hicks. And since they would recognize no authority save that of force, it seemed meet and just to deal with them as they had dealt with us. So Piegan Smith and I stood aloof and watched the grim play, for the fate of a woman hung in the balance. Hicks' salient jaw was set, his expression unreadable.

MacRae stacked the dry wood in a neat pyramid twelve inches from the bare soles of Hicks' feet. He placed the shavings in the edge of the little pile. Then he stood up and began to talk, fingering a match with horrible suggestiveness.

"Perhaps you think that by keeping a close mouth there's a chance to get out of some of the deviltry you've had a hand in lately. But there isn't. You'll get what's coming to you. And in case you're bolstering up your nerve with false hopes in that direction, let me tell you that we know exactly how you turned every trick. I don't particularly care to take the law into my own hands; I'd rather take you in and turn you over to the guard. But there's a woman to account for yet, and so you can take your choice between the same deal you gave Hans Rutter and telling me what became of her."

He paused for a moment. Hicks stared up at him calculatingly.

"I'll tell you all I know about it if you turn me loose," he said. "Give me a horse and a chance to pull my freight, and I'll talk. Otherwise, I'm dumb."

"I'll make no bargains with you," MacRae answered. "Talk or take the consequences."

Hicks shook his head. MacRae coughed—the smoke was still rolling in thick clouds from over the river—and went on.

"Perhaps it will make my meaning clearer if I tell you what happened to Rutter, eh? You and Gregory got him after he was wounded, didn't you? He wouldn't tell where that stuff had been *cached*. But you had a way of loosening a man's tongue—I have you to thank for the idea. Oh, it was a good one, but that old Dutchman was harder stuff than you're made of. You built a fire and warmed his feet. Still he wouldn't talk, so you warmed them some more. Fine! But you didn't suppose you'd ever get *your* feet warmed. I'm not asking much of you, and you'll be no deeper in the mire when you answer. If you don't—well, there's plenty of wood here. Will you tell me what I want to know, or shall I light the fire?"

Still no word from Hicks. MacRae bent and raked the match along a flat stone.

"Oh, well," he said indifferently, "maybe you'll think better of it when your toes begin to sizzle."

He thrust the flaring match among the shavings. As the flame crept in among the broken willows, Hicks raised his head.

"If I tell you what become of her, will you let me go?" he proposed again. "I'll quit the country."

"You'll tell me—or cook by inches, right here," Mac answered deliberately. "You can't buy me off."

The blaze flickered higher. I watched it, with every fiber of my being revolting against such savagery, and the need for it. I glanced at Piegan and Bevans. The one looked on with grim repression, the other with blanched face. And suddenly Hicks jerked up his knees and heaved himself bodily aside with a scream of fear.

"Put it out! Put it out!" he cried. "I'll tell you. For God's sake—anything but the fire!"

"Be quick, then," MacRae muttered, "before I move you back."

"Last night," Hicks gasped, "when we pulled into the gorge to camp, she jerked the six-shooter out uh Lessard's belt and made a run for it. She took to the brush. It was dark, and we couldn't follow her. I don't know where she got to, except that she started down the creek. We hunted for her half the night—didn't see nothin'. That's the truth, s'help me."

"Down the creek—say, by the great Jehosophat!" Piegan exclaimed. "D'yuh remember that racket in the water this mornin'? Yuh wait." He turned and ran down-stream. Almost instantly the smoke had swallowed him.

MacRae stood staring for a second or two, then turned and scattered the fire broadcast on the sand with a movement of his foot. He lifted his hat, and I saw that his forehead and hair was damp with sweat.

"That was a job I had mighty little stomach for," he said, catching my eye and smiling faintly. "I thought that sulky brute would come through if I made a strong bluff. I reckon I'd have weakened in another minute, if he hadn't."

"Ugh!" I shuddered. "It gave me the creeps. I wouldn't make a good Indian."

"Nor I," he agreed. "But I had to know. And I feel better now. I'm not afraid for Lyn, since I know she got away from *them*."

Piegan, at this moment, set up a jubilant hallooing down the river, and shortly came rushing back to us.

"Aha, I told yuh," he cried exultantly. "That was her crossed the river this mornin'. I found her track in the sand. One uh yuh stand guard, and the other feller come with me. We c'n trail her."

"Go ahead," I told MacRae—a superfluous command, for I could not have kept him from going if I had tried.

So I was left on the sand-bar with two dead thieves, and two who should have been dead, and a little knot of horses for company. Hicks and Bevans gave me little concern. I had helped tie both of them, and I knew they would not soon get loose. But it was a weary wait. An hour fled. I paced the bar, a carbine in the crook of my arm and a vigilant eye for incipient outbreaks for freedom on the part of those two wolves. The horses stood about on three legs, heads drooping. The smoke-clouds swayed and eddied, lifted a moment, and closed down again with the varying spasms of the fire that was beating itself out on the farther shore. I sat me down and rested a while, arose and resumed my nervous tramping. The foglike haze began to thin. It became possible to breathe without discomfort to the lungs; my eyes no longer stung and watered. And after a period in which I seemed to have walked a thousand miles on that sandy point, I heard voices in the distance. Presently MacRae and Piegan Smith broke through the willow fringe on the higher ground—and with them appeared a feminine figure that waved a hand to me.

CHAPTER XXIII.

THE SPOILS OF WAR.

All things considered, it was a joyous knot of humanity that gathered on that sand-bar—if one excepts the two plunderers who were tied hard and fast, their most cheerful outlook a speedy trial with a hangman's noose at the finish. I recollect that we shook hands all around, and that our tongues wagged extravagantly, regardless of whoever else might be speaking. We settled down before long, however, remembering that we were not altogether out of the woods.

The fire by this time had, to a great extent, beaten itself out on the opposite bank, and with nothing left but a few smoldering brush-patches, the smoke continued to lift and give us sundry glimpses of the black desolation that spread to the north. So far as we knew, the wind had carried no sparks across the river to fire the south side and drive us back to the barrenness of the burned lands. And with the certainty that Lyn was safe, and that we were beyond disputing masters of the situation, came consciousness of hunger and great bodily weariness. It was almost twenty-four hours since we had eaten, and we were simply ravenous. As a start toward an orderly method of procedure, we began by re-dressing Piegan's punctured arm, which had begun to bleed again; though it was by no means as serious a hurt as it might have been. Piegan himself seemed to consider it a good deal of a joke on him, and when I remarked that I failed to see how a bullet-hole through any part of one's person could be regarded in a humorous light, Piegan snorted, and told me that I would know more when I grew up. A little ventilation, he declared, was something a man's system needed every year or two.

Then we unsaddled and unpacked the horses, and moved them up on the grassy flat. Piegan elected himself guard over the prisoners, while the rest of us cooked a belated breakfast, and he assured them repeatedly that he would be delighted to have them make a break, so that he could have the pleasure of perforating their individual and collective hides. I really believe the old rascal meant it, too; he succeeded, at least, in giving that impression, and his crippled arm was no handicap to him—he could juggle a six-shooter right or left-handed with amazing dexterity.

Lyn substantiated Goodell's story in every detail, so far as it had dealt with her, and she told me, while we pottered about the fire, how she waited her chance when they made camp in Sage Creek, and, snatching Lessard's gun, ran for it in the dark.

"I didn't really know where I was," she told me naively. "So I thought I'd better hide till daylight and watch them go before I started. Then I could try and make my way back to the freight outfit—I felt sure they would either wait for me or send a man back to Walsh when I didn't come back. I was hiding in those cottonwoods when you came stealing in there this morning. You were so quiet, I couldn't tell who it was—I thought perhaps they were still hunting for me; they did, you know—they were rummaging around after me for a long time. But I never dreamed it could be you and Gordon. So I sneaked down to the river and crossed; I was deadly afraid they'd find me, and I thought once I was on the other side I could hear them coming, and scuttle away in the brush. Then about daylight I heard some shooting, and wondered if they had been followed. I didn't dare cross the river and start over the hills with that fire coming, and the smoke so thick I couldn't tell a hill from a hollow. I waited a while longer—I was in this brush up here"—she pointed to a place almost opposite—"and in a little while I heard more shooting, and in a minute or so, he"—indicating Hicks—"came splashing through the river. He was on the sand-bar before I could see him clearly, and coming straight toward where I was huddled in the brush. Oh, but I was frightened, and before I knew it, almost, I poked the gun between the branches and fired at his head as straight as I could—and he fell off his horse. Then I ran, before any more of them came. And that's really all there is to it. I was plodding up the river, when I heard Gordon shouting two or three hundred yards behind. Of course I knew his voice, and stopped. But dear me! this seems like a bad dream, or maybe I ought to say a good one. I hope you won't all disappear in the smoke."

155

"Don't you worry," MacRae assured her. "When we vanish in the smoke we'll take you with us."

After we had eaten we made a systematic search of packs and saddle-pockets, and when we had finished there was more of the root of all evil in sight than I have laid my eyes on at any one time before or since. The gold that had drawn us into the game was there in the same long, buckskin sacks, a load for one horse. The government money, looted from the paymaster, part gold coin and part bills, they had divided, and it was stowed in various places. Lessard's saddle-pockets were crammed, and likewise those of Hicks and Gregory. Bevans' *anqueros*, which I had taken from his dead horse, yielded a goodly sum. Altogether, we counted some seventy-odd thousand dollars, exclusive of the gold-dust in the sacks.

"There's a good deal more than that, according to Goodell's figures," MacRae commented. "Lessard must have got away with quite a sum from the post. I daresay the pockets of the combination hold the rest. But I don't hanker to search a dead man, and that can wait till we get to Walsh."

"Yuh goin' t' lug this coyote bait t' Fort Walsh?" Piegan inquired. "I'd leave 'em right here without the ceremony uh plantin'. An' I vote right here an' now t' neck these other two geesers together an' run 'em off'n a high bank into deep water."

"I'd vote with you, so far as my personal feeling in the matter goes," MacRae replied. "But we've got a lot of mighty black marks against us, right now, and we're going in there to relate a most amazing tale. Of course, we can prove every word of it. But I reckon we'll have to take these two carcasses along as a sort of corroborative evidence. Every confounded captain in the Force will have to view them officially; they wouldn't take our word for their being dead. So it would only delay the clearing up of things to leave them here. These other jaspers will lend a fine decorative effect to the noosed end of a three-quarter-inch rope for their part in the play—unless Canadian justice miscarries, which doesn't often happen if you give it time enough to get at the root of things."

Much as we had accomplished, we still had a problem or two ahead of us. While we didn't reckon on having to defend ourselves against the preposterous charge of holding up the paymaster, there was that little matter of violent assault on the persons of three uniformed representatives of Northwestern law—assault, indeed, with deadly weapons; also the forcible sequestration of government property in the shape of three troop-horses with complete riding appurtenances; the uttering of threats; all of which was strictly against the peace and dignity of the Crown and the statutes made and provided. No man is supposed, as MacRae had pointed out to me after we'd held up those three troopers, to inflict a compound fracture on one law in his efforts to preserve another. But it had been necessary for us to do so, and we had justified our judgment in playing a lone hand and upsetting Lessard's smoothly conceived plan to lay us by the heels while he and his thugs got away with the plunder. We had broken up as hard a combination as ever matched itself against the scarlet-coated keepers of the law; we had gathered them in with the loot intact, and for this signal service we had hopes that the powers that be would overlook the break we made on Lost River ridge. Lessard had created a damnatory piece of evidence against himself by lifting the post funds; that in itself would bear witness to the truth of our story. It might take the authorities a while to get the proper focus on the tangle, but we could stand that, seeing that we had won against staggering odds.

From the mouth of Sage Creek to Fort Walsh it is a fraction over fifty miles, across comparatively flat country. By the time our breakfast was done we calculated it to be ten o'clock. We had the half of a long mid-summer day to make it. So, partly because we might find the full fifty miles an ash-strewn waste, fodderless, blackened, where an afternoon halt would be a dreary sojourn, and partly for the sake of the three good horses we had pushed so unmercifully through the early hours of the night, we laid on the grassy river-bottom till noon. Then we packed, placed the sullen captives in the saddle with hands lashed stoutly, mounted our horses and recrossed the river. Once on the uplands we struck the long trot—eight hours of daylight to make fifty miles. And we made it.

CHAPTER XXIV.

THE PIPE OF PEACE.

Twenty minutes after the sunset gun awoke the echoes along Battle Creek we slipped quietly into Fort Walsh and drew rein before the official quarters of the officer of the day; a stiffened, saddle-weary group, grimy with the sooty ash of burned prairies. From the near-by barracks troopers craned through windows, and gathered in doorways. For a moment I thought the office was deserted, but before we had time to dismount, the captain ranking next to Lessard appeared from within, and behind him came a medium-sized man, gray-haired and pleasant of countenance, at sight of whom MacRae straightened in his saddle with a stifled exclamation and repeated the military salute.

The captain stared in frank astonishment as MacRae got stiffly out of his saddle and helped Lyn to the ground. Then he snapped out some sharp question, but the gray-haired one silenced him with a gesture.

"Softly, softly, Stone," he said. "Let the man explain voluntarily."

"Beg to report, sir," MacRae began evenly, "that we have captured the men who robbed Flood, murdered those two miners, and held up the paymaster. Also that we have recovered all the stolen money."

"What sort of cock-and-bull story is this?" Stone broke in angrily. "Preposterous! Orderly, call— —"

"Easy, easy now, Captain Stone," the older man cut in sharply. "A man doesn't make a statement like that without some proof. By the way," he asked abruptly, "how did you manage to elude Major Lessard and get in here?"

MacRae pointed to one of the horses. "We didn't elude him. You'll find what's left of the black-hearted devil under that canvas," he answered coolly. "Lessard was at the bottom of the crookedness. We've packed him and Paul Gregory fifty miles for you to see."

"Ha!" the old fellow seemed not so surprised as I had expected. He glanced over the lot of us and let another long-drawn "ha" escape.

"May I ask a favor, Colonel Allen?" MacRae continued. "This lady has had a hard day. Will you excuse her, for the present? We have a story to tell that you may find hard to credit."

The colonel (I'd heard of him before; I knew when MacRae spoke his name that he was Commander-in-Chief of the Northwest Mounted Police, the biggest gun of all) favored us with another appraising stare.

"These men, I take it, are prisoners?" he said, pointing to Hicks and Bevans.

"You bet your sweet life them's prisoners," Piegan broke in with cheerful assurance. "Them gentlemen is candidates for a rope necktie apiece—nice perfessional assassins t' have in the Police!"

Allen turned to the orderly. "A detail of four from the guardhouse on the double-quick," he commanded.

Captain Stone stood by gnawing his mustache while Allen listened unmoved as MacRae pointed out the horse on which was packed the bulk of the loot, and gave him a brief outline of the abduction and the subsequent fight at the mouth of Sage Creek. The orderly returned with the detail, and Allen courteously sent him to escort Lyn to the hospitality of Bat Perkins' wife, as MacRae asked. After which the guard marshaled Piegan, MacRae, and me, along with Hicks and Bevans, into the room where MacRae and Lessard had clashed that memorable day. Then they carried in the two bodies and laid them on the floor, and last of all the pack that held Hank Rowan's gold and the government currency.

While this was being done an orderly flitted from house to house on officers' row; the calm, pleasant-voiced, shrewd old Commissioner gathered his captains about him for a semi-official hearing. The dusk faded into night. Here and there about the post lights began to twinkle. We stood about in the ante-room, silent under the vigilant eye of the guard. After an uncertain period of waiting, the orderly called "Gordon MacRae," and the inquisition began.

One at a time they put us on the rack—probing each man's story down to the smallest detail. It was long after midnight when the questioning was at an end. The finale came when a trooper searched the bodies of Lessard and Gregory, and relieved Hicks and Bevans of the plunder that was still concealed about their persons. They counted the money solemnly, on the same desk by which Lessard stood when MacRae flung that hot challenge in his teeth, and lost his stripes as the penalty. Outside, the wind arose and whoo-*ee*-ed around the corner of the log building; inside, there was a strained quiet, broken only by the occasional rattle of a loose window, the steady chink—chink of coin slipping through fingers, the crisp rustle of bills, like new silk. And when it was done Allen leaned back in his chair, patting the arm of it with one hand, and surveyed the neatly piled money and the three buckskin sacks on the desk before him. Then he stood up, very erect and stern in the yellow lamplight.

"Take those men to the guardhouse," he ordered curtly, pointing an accusing finger at Hicks and Bevans. "Iron them securely— securely!"

He turned to me. "I regret that it will be necessary for you to wait some little time, Flood, before your money can be restored to you," he said in a pleasanter tone. "There will be certain formalities to go through, you understand. You will also be required as a witness at the forthcoming trial. We shall be glad to furnish you and Smith with comfortable quarters until then. It is late, but MacRae knows these barracks, and doubtless he can find you a temporary sleeping place. And, in conclusion, I wish to compliment all three of you on the courage and resource you displayed in tracking down these damnable scoundrels—*damnable* scoundrels."

He fairly exploded that last phrase. I daresay it was something of a blow to his pride in the Force to learn that such deviltry had actually been fathered by one of his trusted officers; something the same sorrowful anger that stirs a man when one of his own kin goes wrong. Then, as if he were half-ashamed of his burst of feeling, he dismissed us with a wave of his hand and a gruff "That's all, to-night."

That practically was the finish of the thing. There was, of course, a trial, at which Hicks and Bevans were convicted out of hand and duly sentenced to be hung—a sentence that was carried out with neatness and despatch in the near future. Also, I did manage, in the fullness of time, to deliver La Pere's ten thousand dollars without further gun-play.

Colonel Allen knew a good man when he saw one—he was not long in demonstrating that fact. When everything was straightened out, MacRae—urged thereto by Lyn—made a straightforward request for honorable discharge But he did not get it. Instead, the gray-haired Commissioner calmly offered him promotion to an Inspectorship, which is equivalent to the rank of a captain, and carries pay of two thousand a year. And MacRae, of course, accepted.

The day he cast off the old red jacket of the rank and file and put on the black uniform with braid looped back and forth across the front of it, and gold hieroglyphics on the collar, Piegan Smith and I stood up with him and Lyn and helped them get fitted to double harness. Not that there was any lack of other folk; indeed, it seemed to me that the official contingent of Fort Walsh had turned out en masse to attend the ceremony. But Piegan and I were the star guests.

Ah, well, we can't always be young and full of the pure joy of living. One must grow old. And inevitably one looks back with a pang, and sighs for the vanished days. But Time keeps his scythe a-swinging, and we go out—like a snuffed candle. We *lived*, though, we who frolicked along the forty-ninth parallel when Civilization stood afar and viewed the scene askance; but she came down upon us and took possession fast enough when that wild land was partly tamed, and now few are left of those who knew and loved the old West, its perils, its hardships, its bigness of heart and readiness of hand. Such of us as remain are like the buffalo penned in national parks—a sorry remnant of the days that were.

THE END.